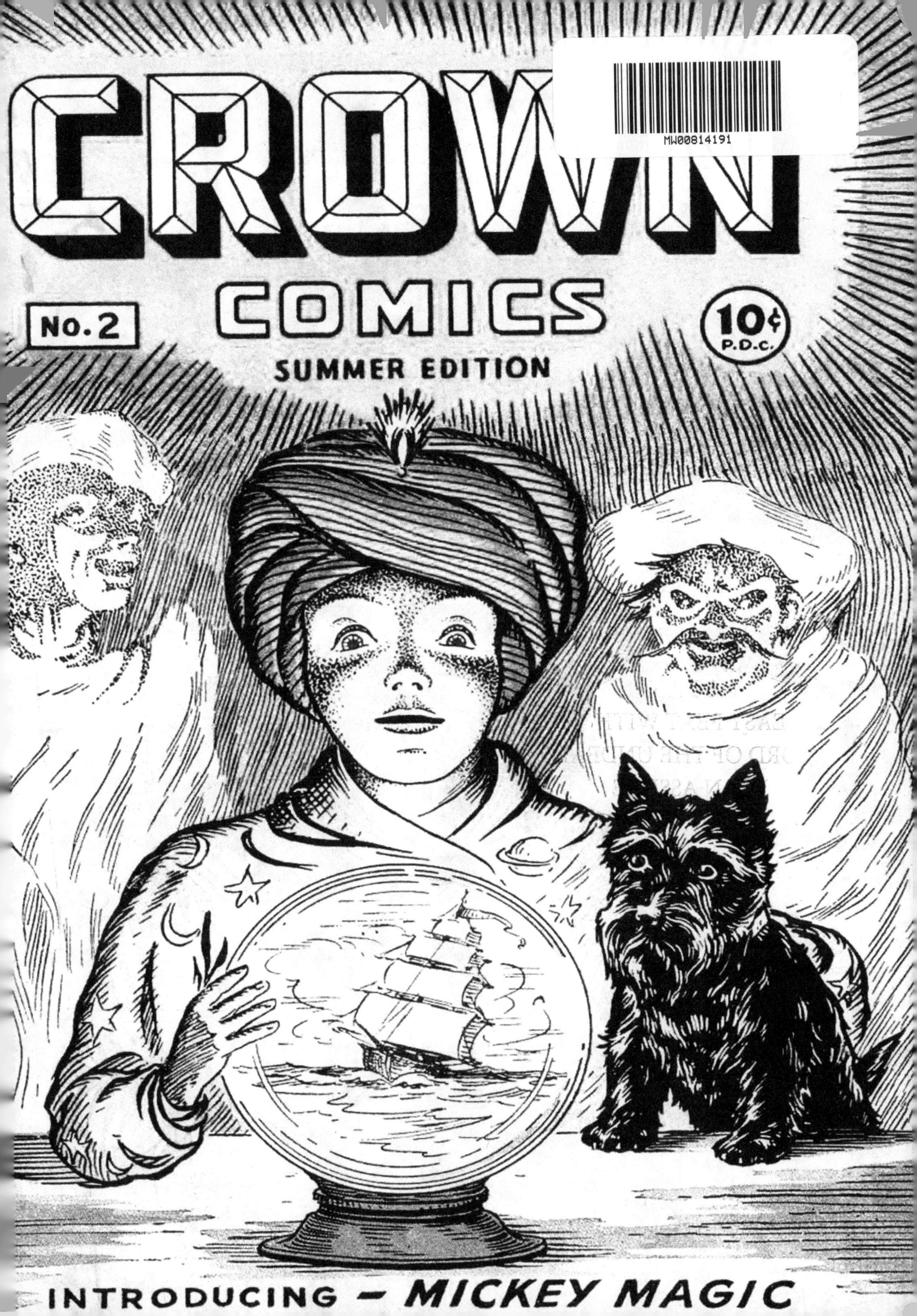
CROWN
COMICS
No. 2
10¢
P.D.C.
SUMMER EDITION
INTRODUCING – MICKEY MAGIC

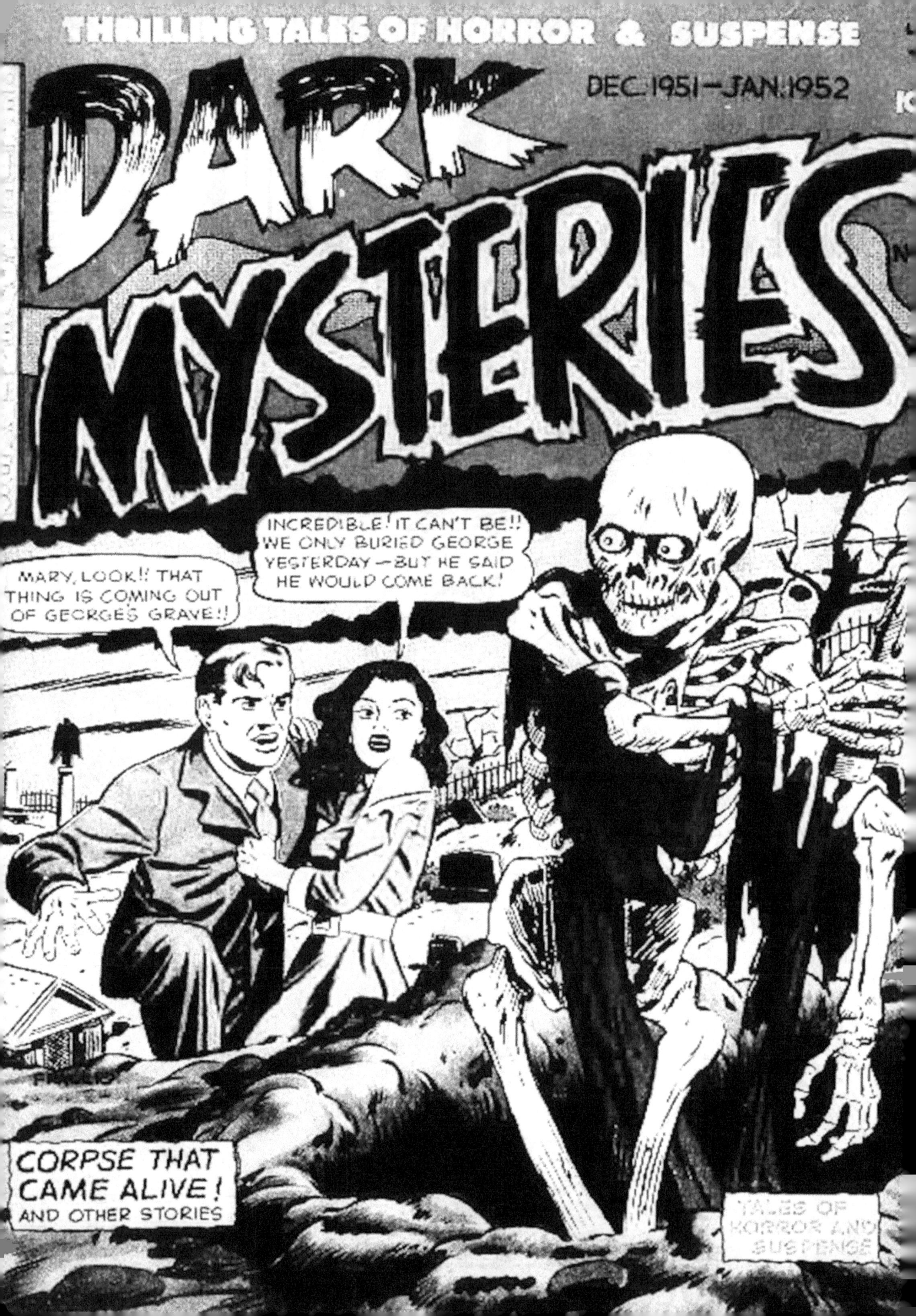
THRILLING TALES OF HORROR & SUSPENSE
DARK MYSTERIES
DEC. 1951—JAN. 1952
MARY, LOOK!! THAT THING IS COMING OUT OF GEORGE'S GRAVE!!
INCREDIBLE! IT CAN'T BE!! WE ONLY BURIED GEORGE YESTERDAY—BUT HE SAID HE WOULD COME BACK!
CORPSE THAT CAME ALIVE! AND OTHER STORIES
TALES OF HORROR AND SUSPENSE

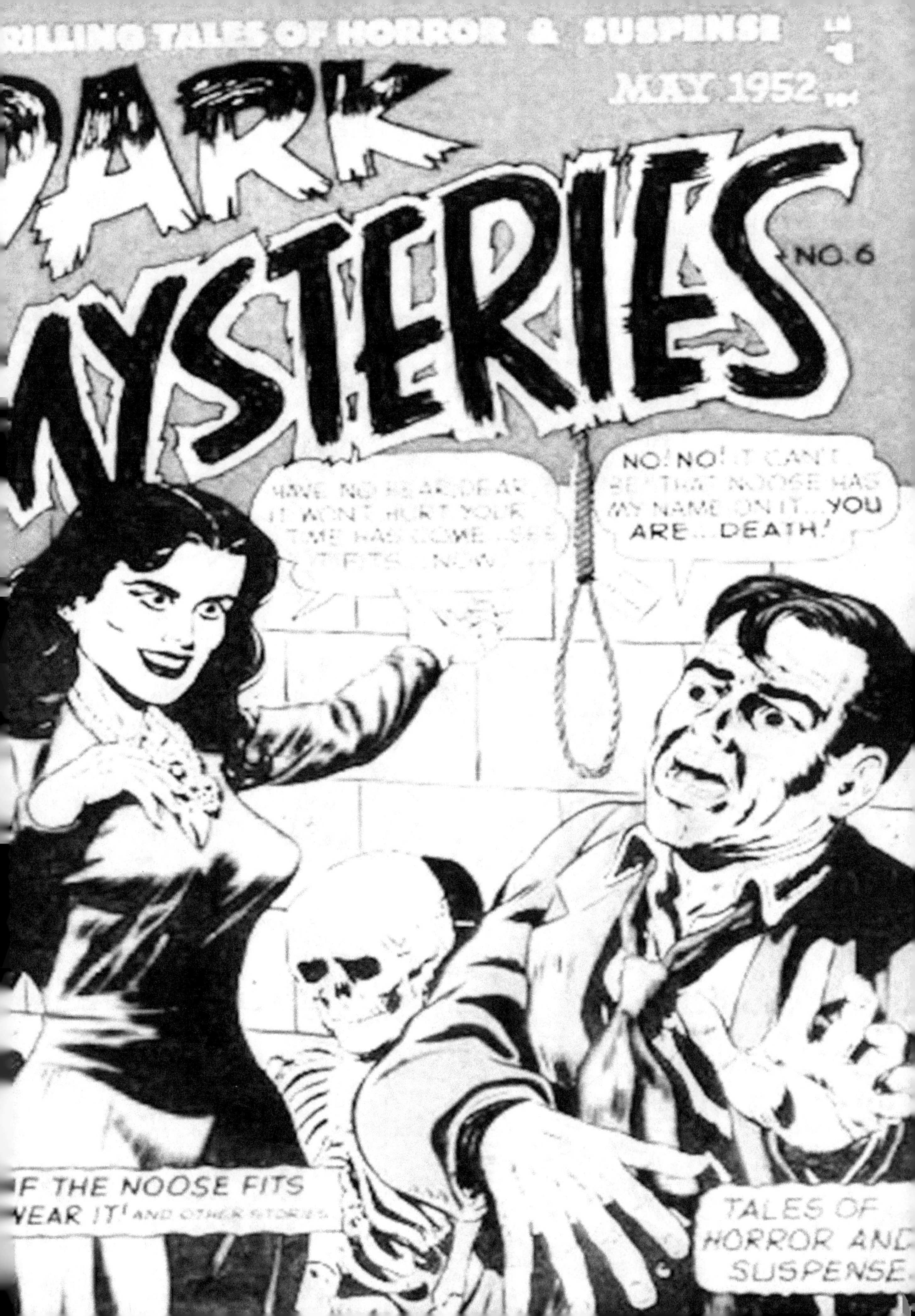
RILLING TALES OF HORROR & SUSPENSE
MAY 1952
10¢
DARK MYSTERIES
NO. 6
NO! NO! IT CAN'T BE! THAT NOOSE HAS MY NAME ON IT... YOU ARE... DEATH!
F THE NOOSE FITS
EAR IT! AND OTHER STORIES
TALES OF HORROR AND SUSPENSE

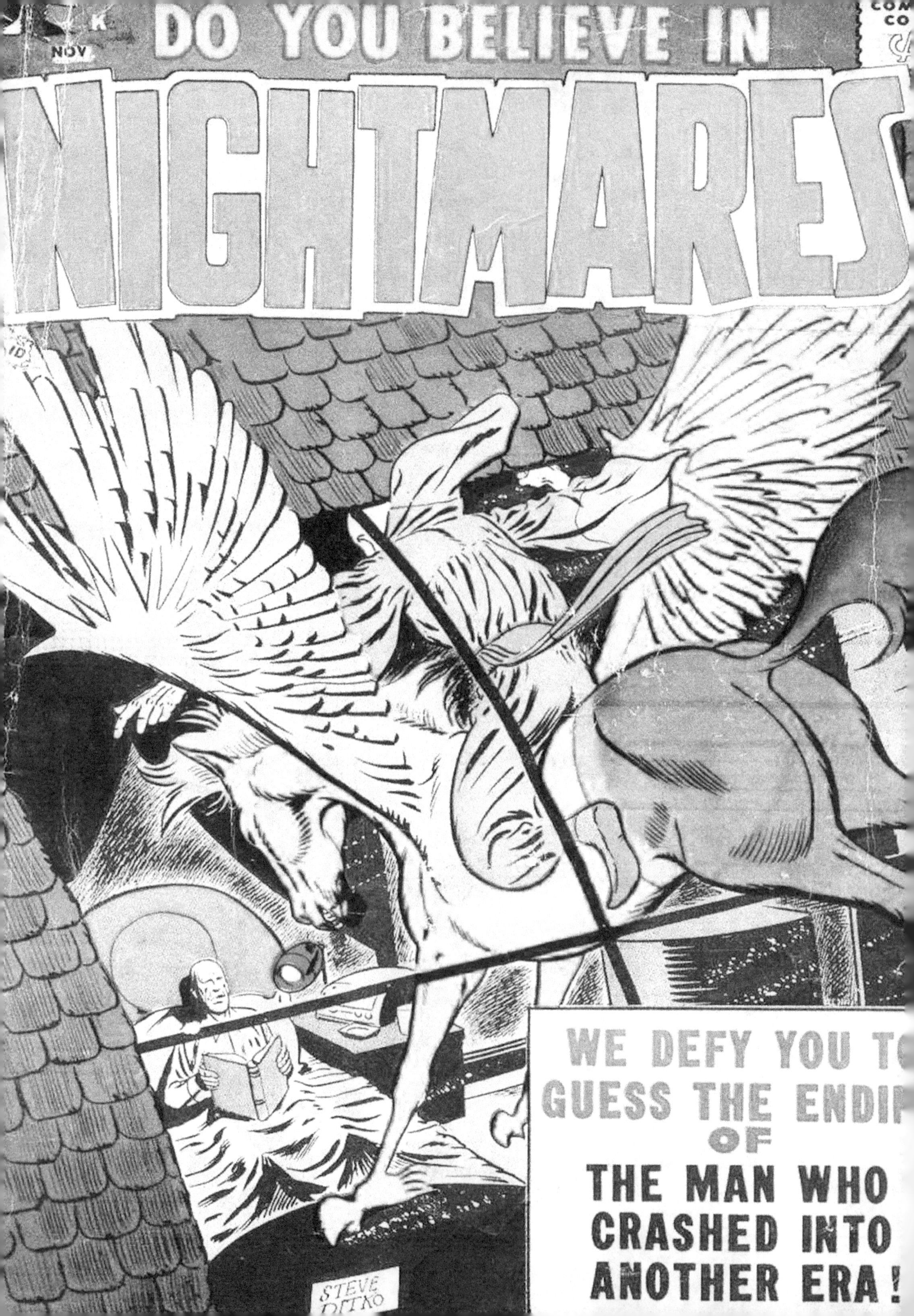
NOV
DO YOU BELIEVE IN
NIGHTMARES
WE DEFY YOU T
GUESS THE ENDI
OF
THE MAN WHO
CRASHED INTO
ANOTHER ERA!
STEVE
DITKO

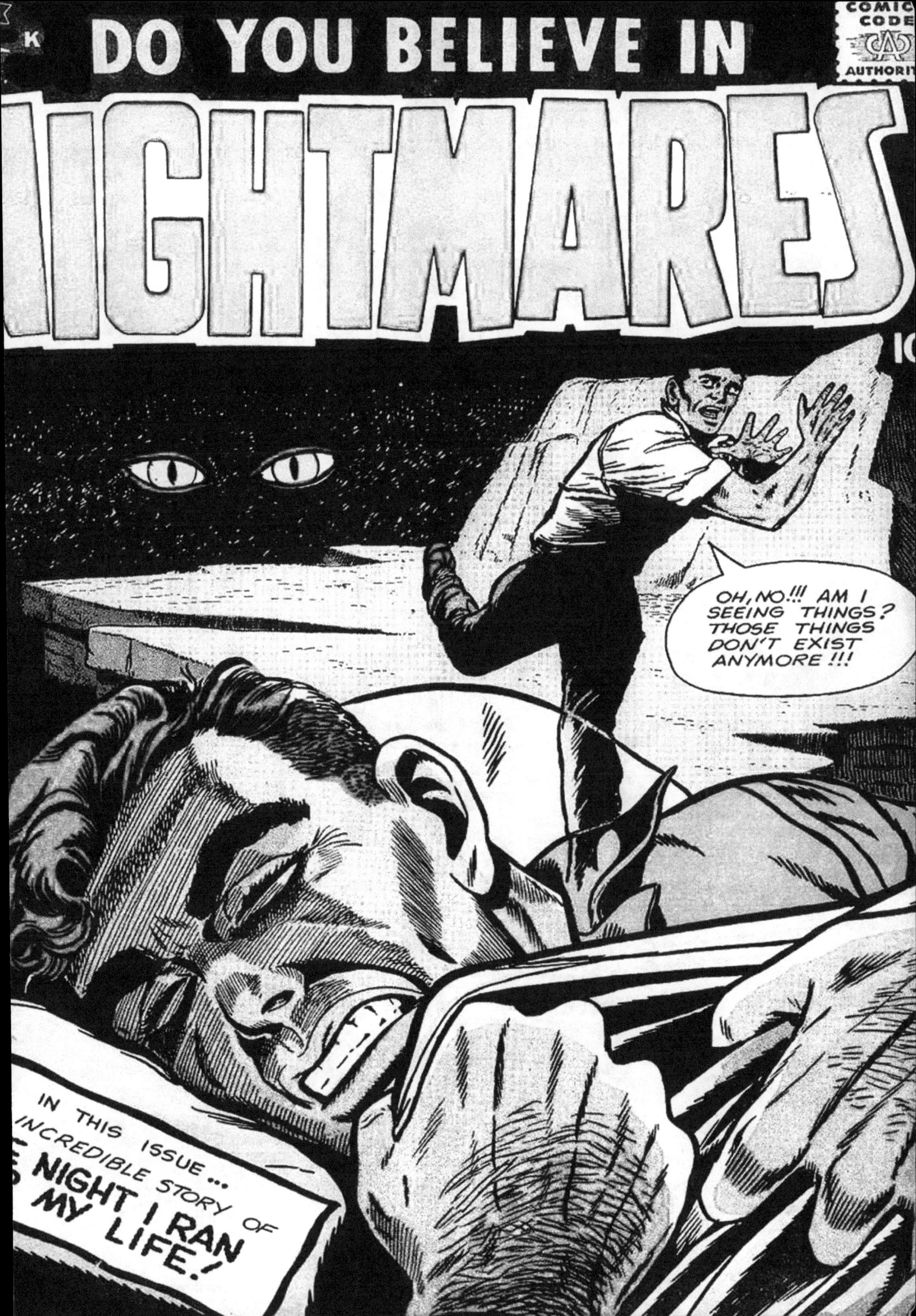
DO YOU BELIEVE IN
IGHTMARES
OH, NO!!! AM I SEEING THINGS? THOSE THINGS DON'T EXIST ANYMORE!!!
IN THIS ISSUE... INCREDIBLE STORY OF
E NIGHT I RAN
S MY LIFE!

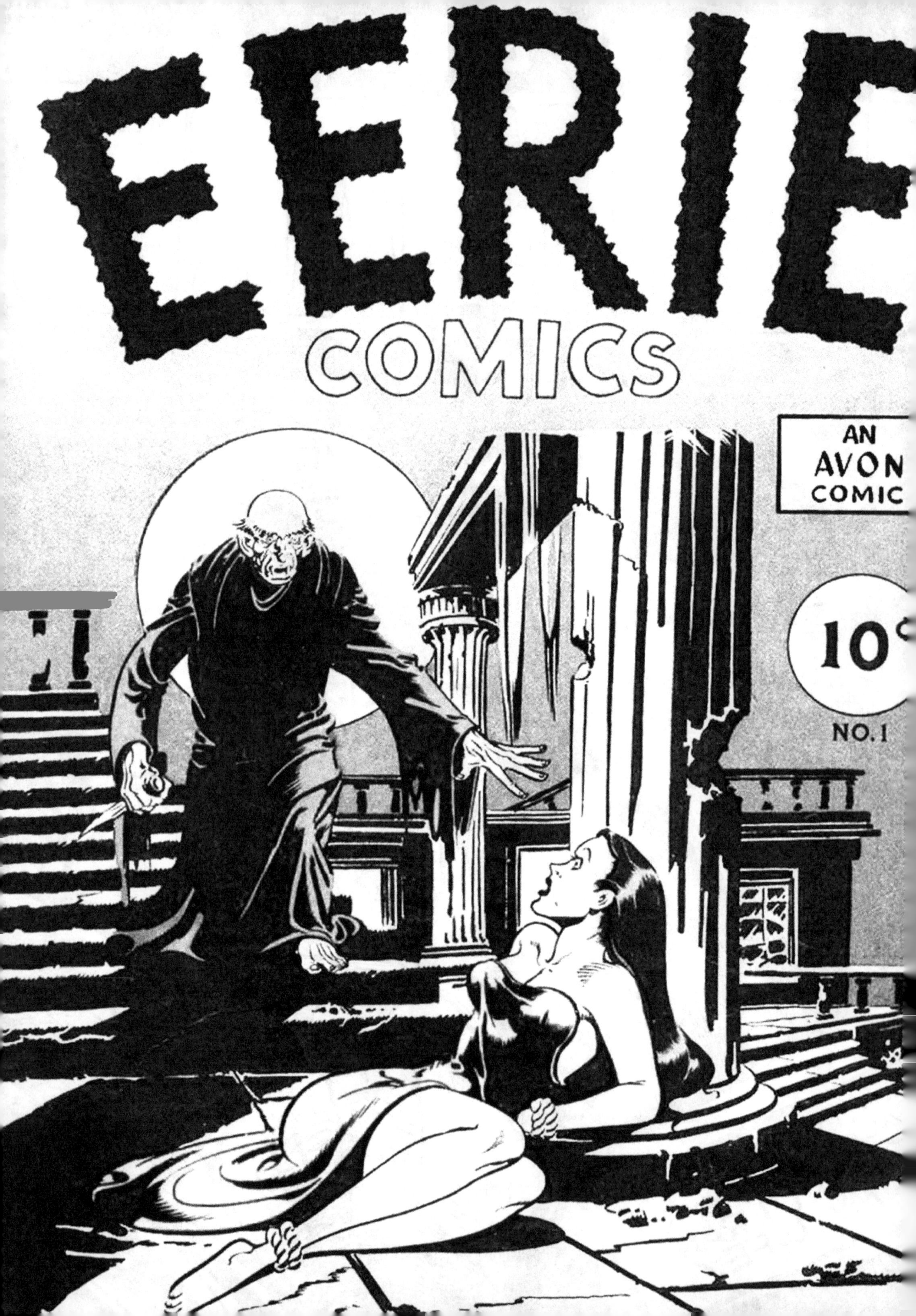

EERIE
COMICS
AN AVON COMIC
10¢
NO. 1

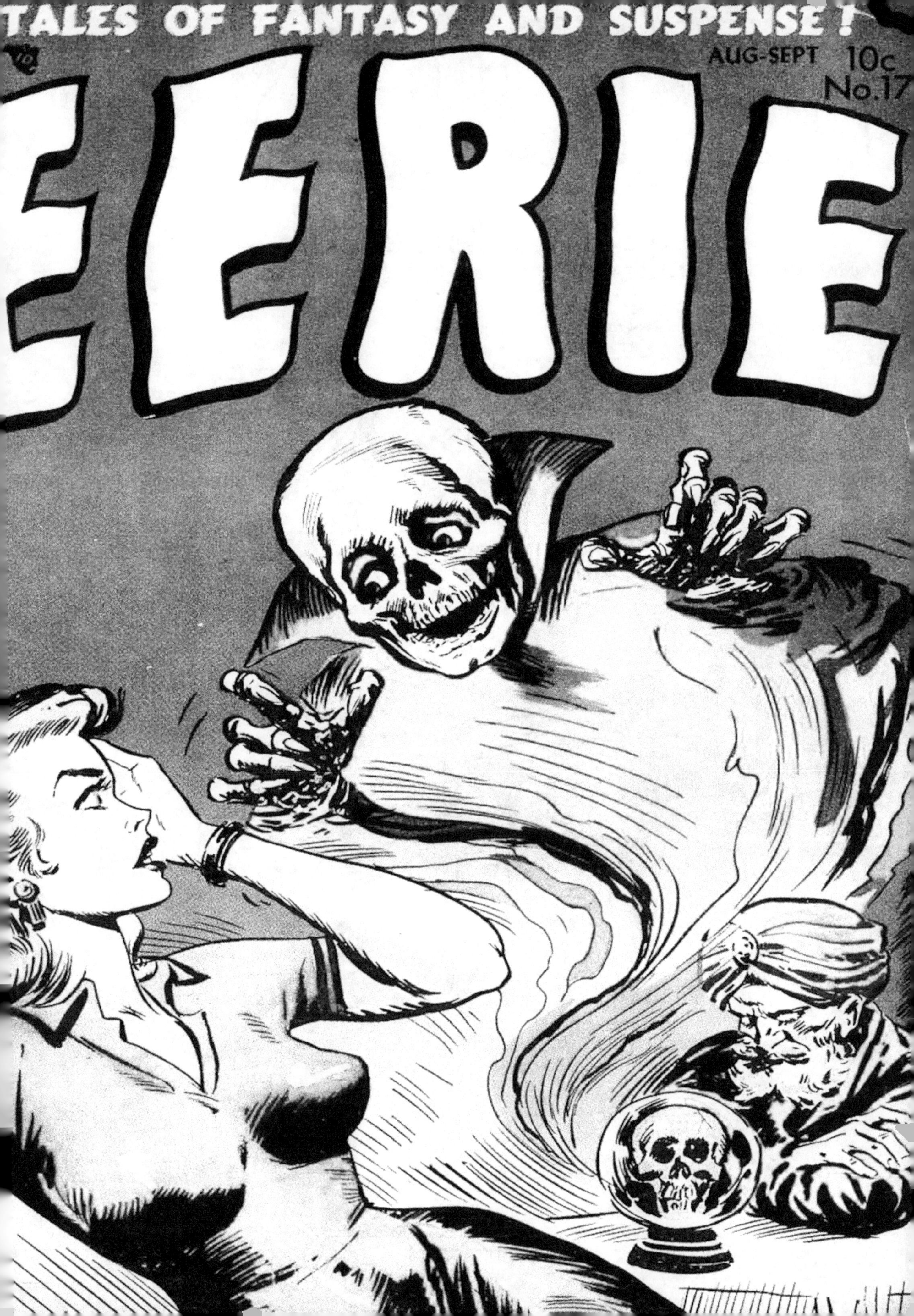
TALES OF FANTASY AND SUSPENSE!
AUG-SEPT
10c
No.17
EERIE

ANC

EXPOSED

TRUE CRIME CASES

Vol. I No. 1 1C

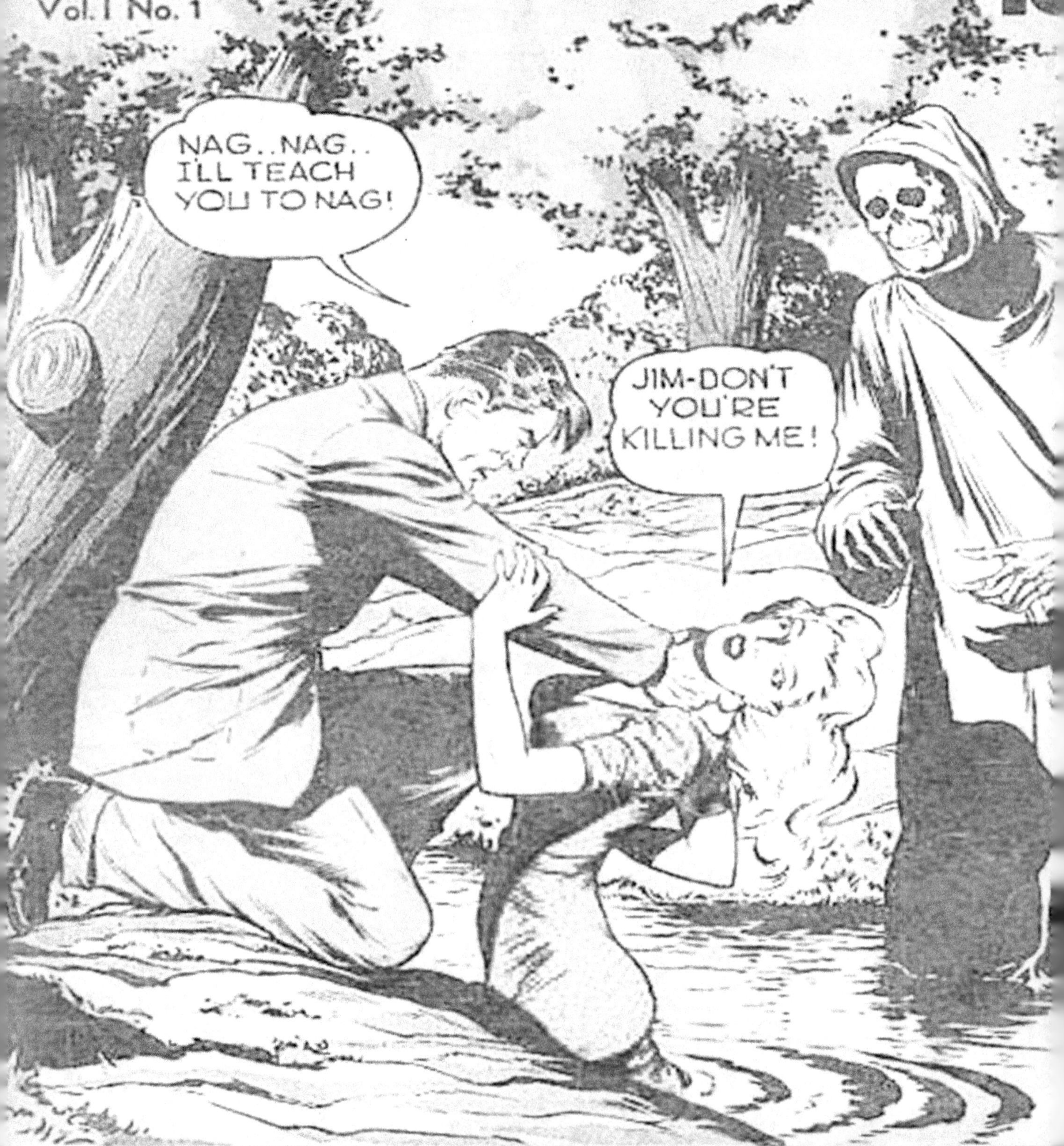
NAG..NAG..
I'LL TEACH
YOU TO NAG!
JIM-DON'T
YOU'RE
KILLING ME!

CORPSES CASH AND CARRY – DEATH THUMBS A
INSIDE WITNESS – LEGEND of the LONE WO

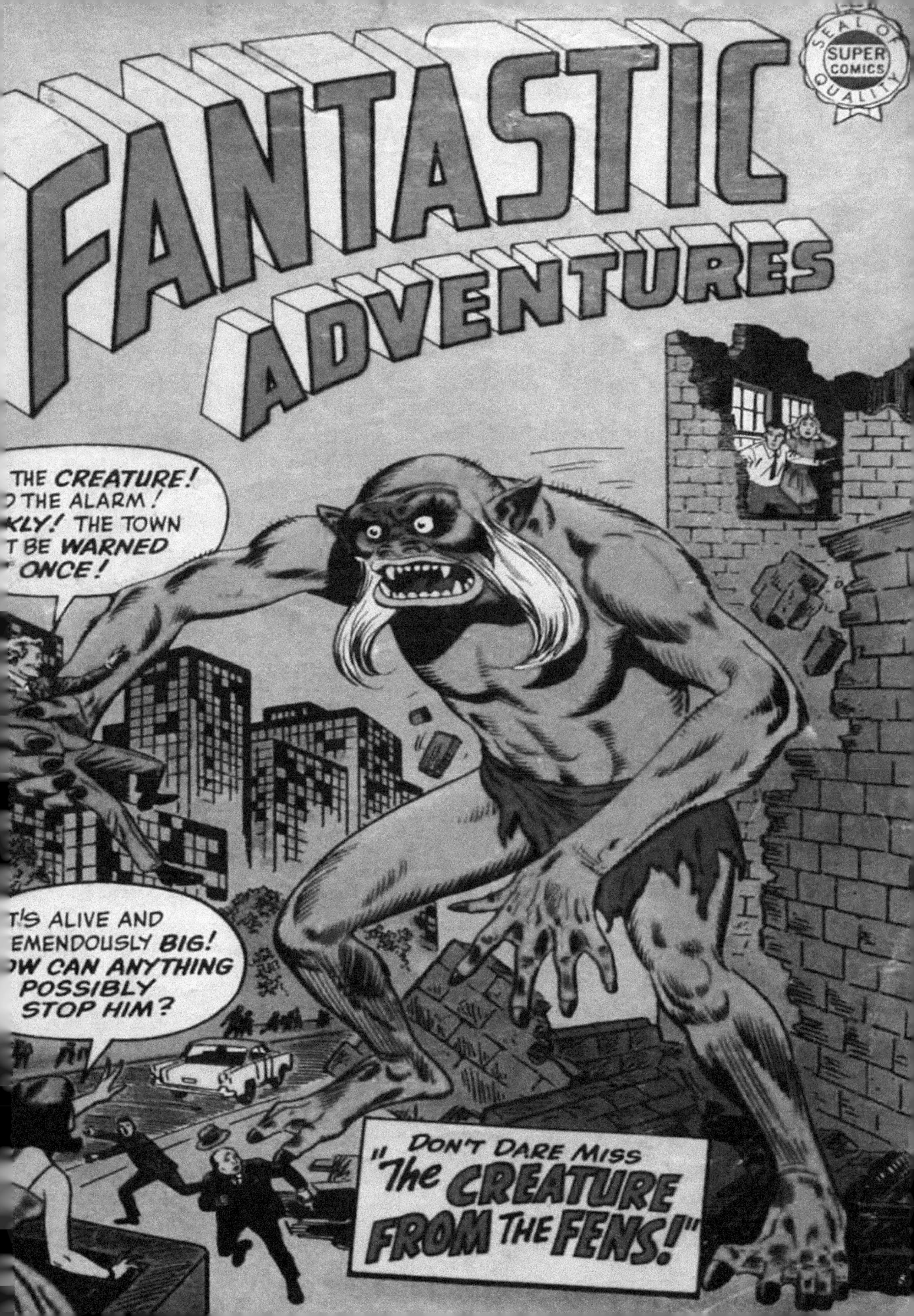
FANTASTIC ADVENTURES
SEAL OF SUPER COMICS QUALITY
THE CREATURE!
THE ALARM!
KLY! THE TOWN
T BE WARNED
ONCE!
T'S ALIVE AND
EMENDOUSLY BIG!
OW CAN ANYTHING
POSSIBLY
STOP HIM?
DON'T DARE MISS
"The CREATURE FROM THE FENS!"

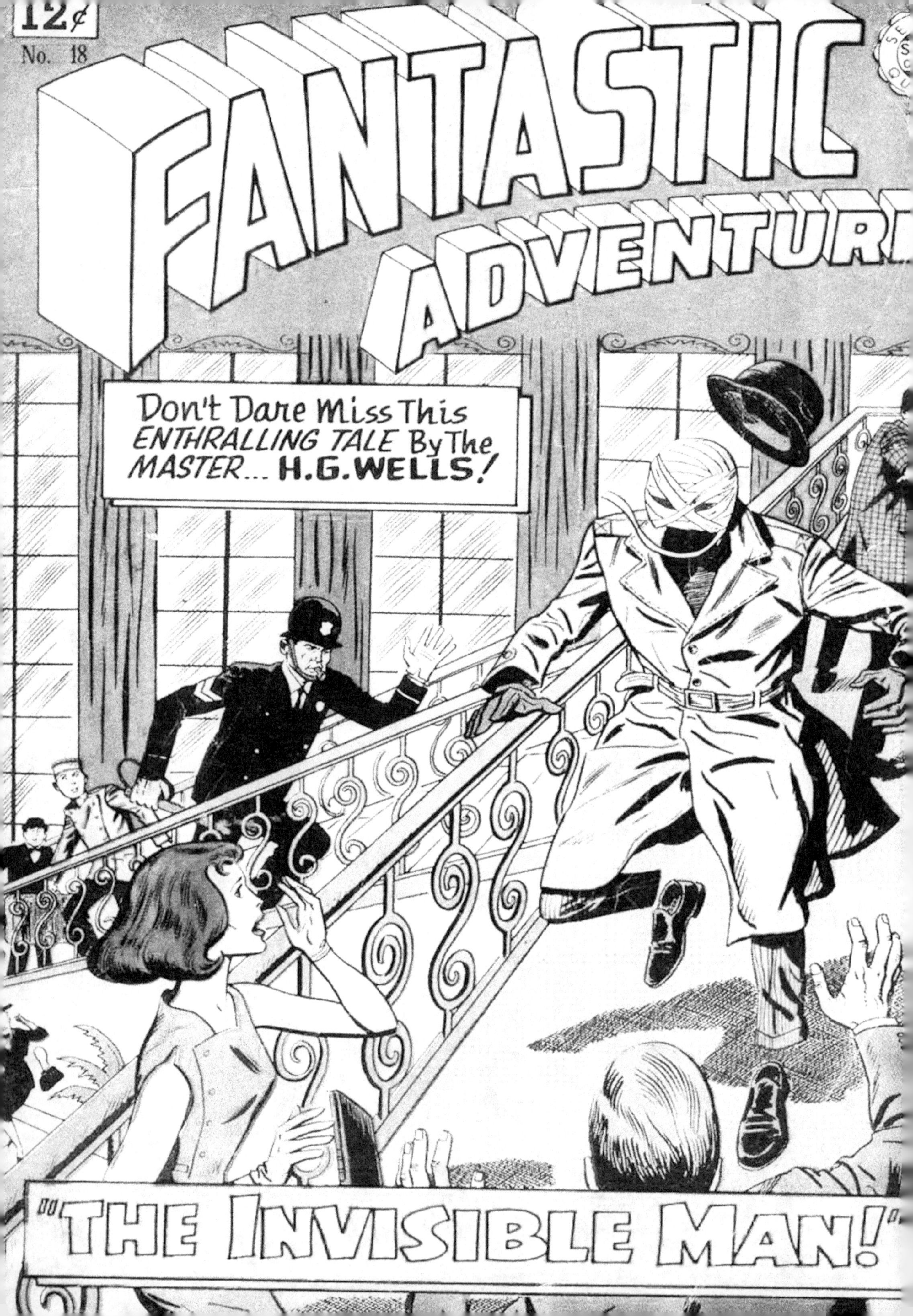
12¢
No. 18
FANTASTIC ADVENTURES
Don't Dare Miss This ENTHRALLING TALE By The MASTER... H.G. WELLS!
"THE INVISIBLE MAN!"

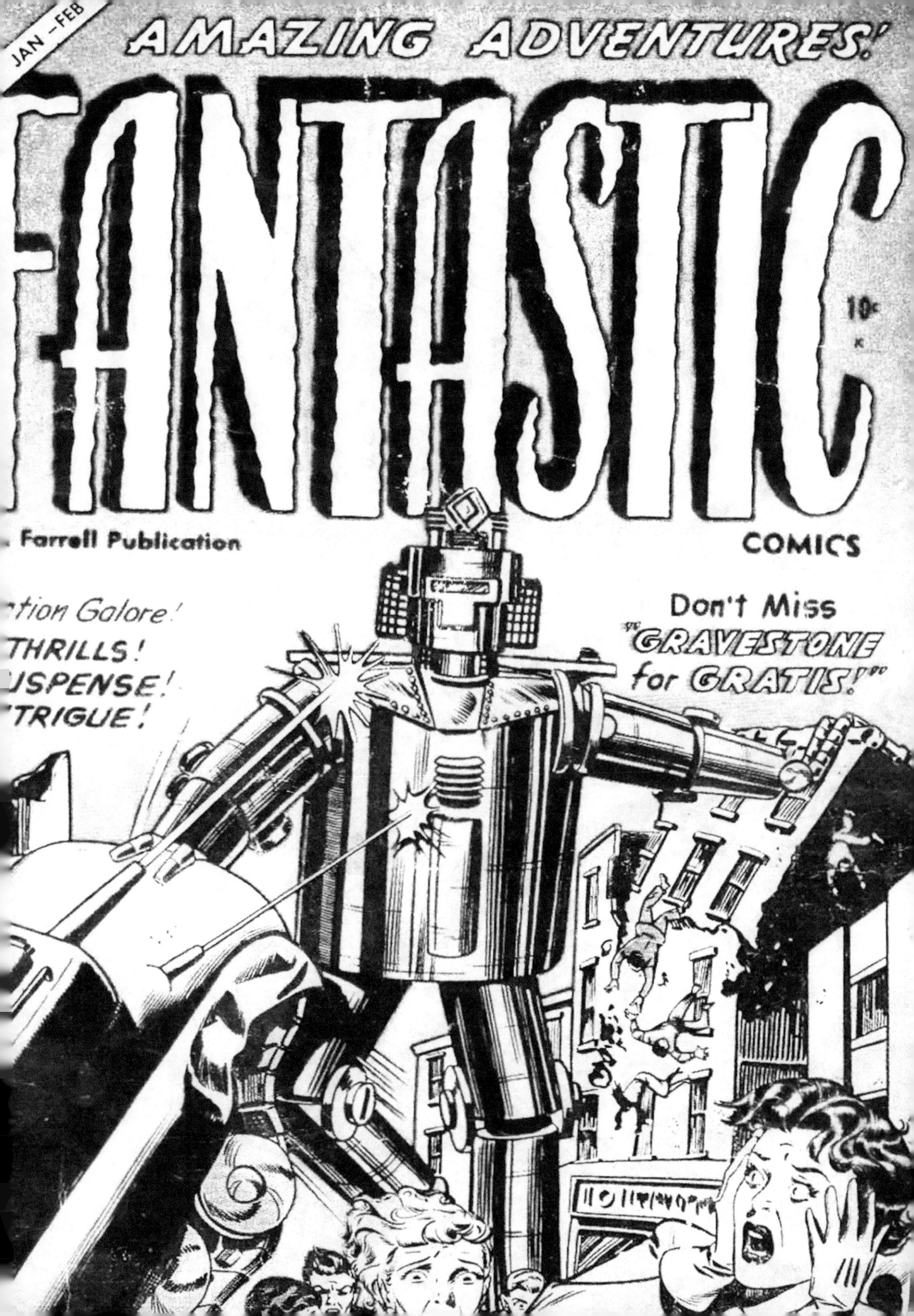
JAN – FEB
AMAZING ADVENTURES!
FANTASTIC
10¢
Farrell Publication
COMICS
tion Galore!
THRILLS!
USPENSE!
TRIGUE!
Don't Miss
"GRAVESTONE for GRATIS!"

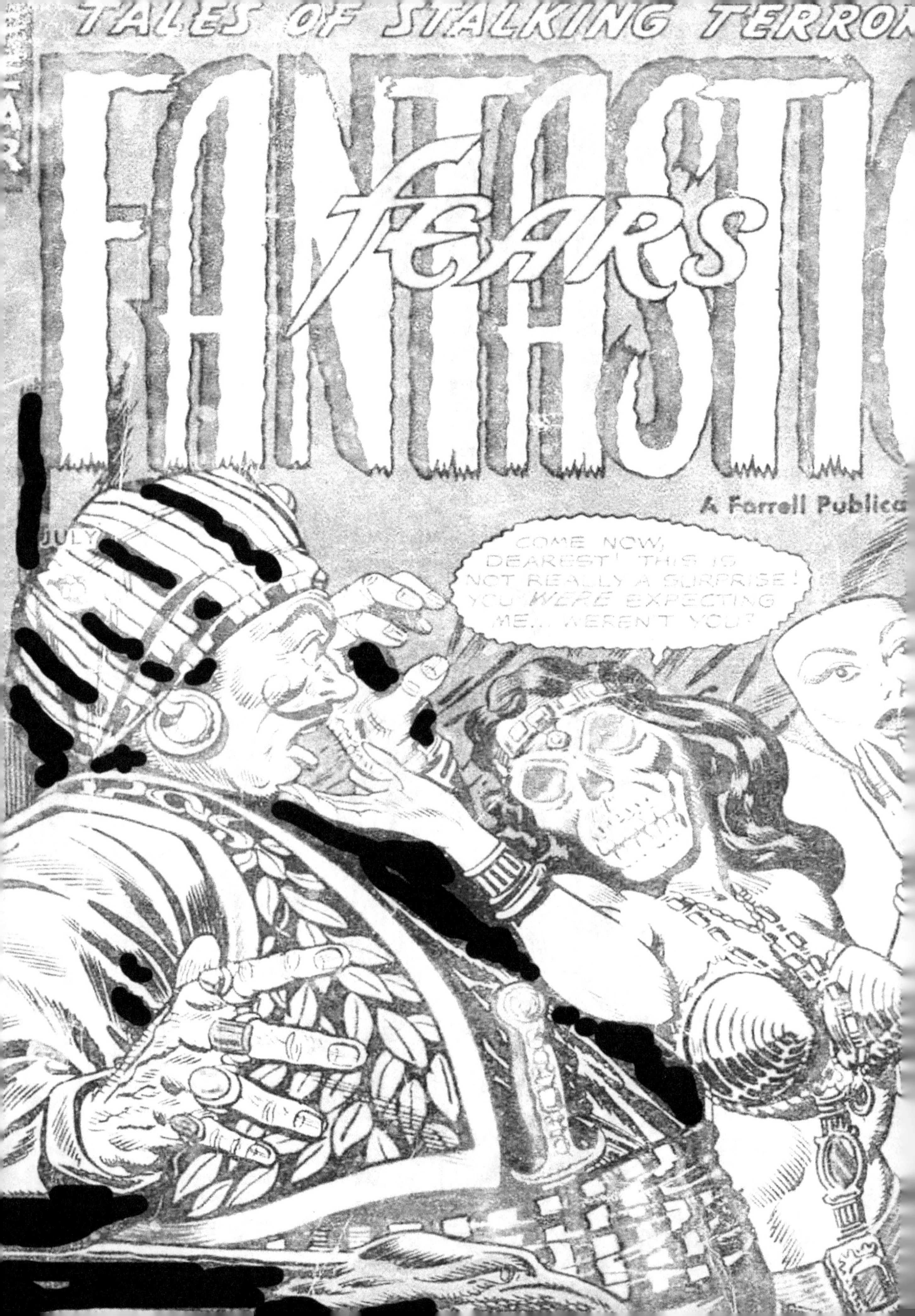
TALES OF STALKING TERROR
FANTASTIC
fears
A Farrell Publica
JULY
COME NOW, DEAREST! THIS IS NOT REALLY A SURPRISE! YOU WERE EXPECTING ME... WEREN'T YOU?

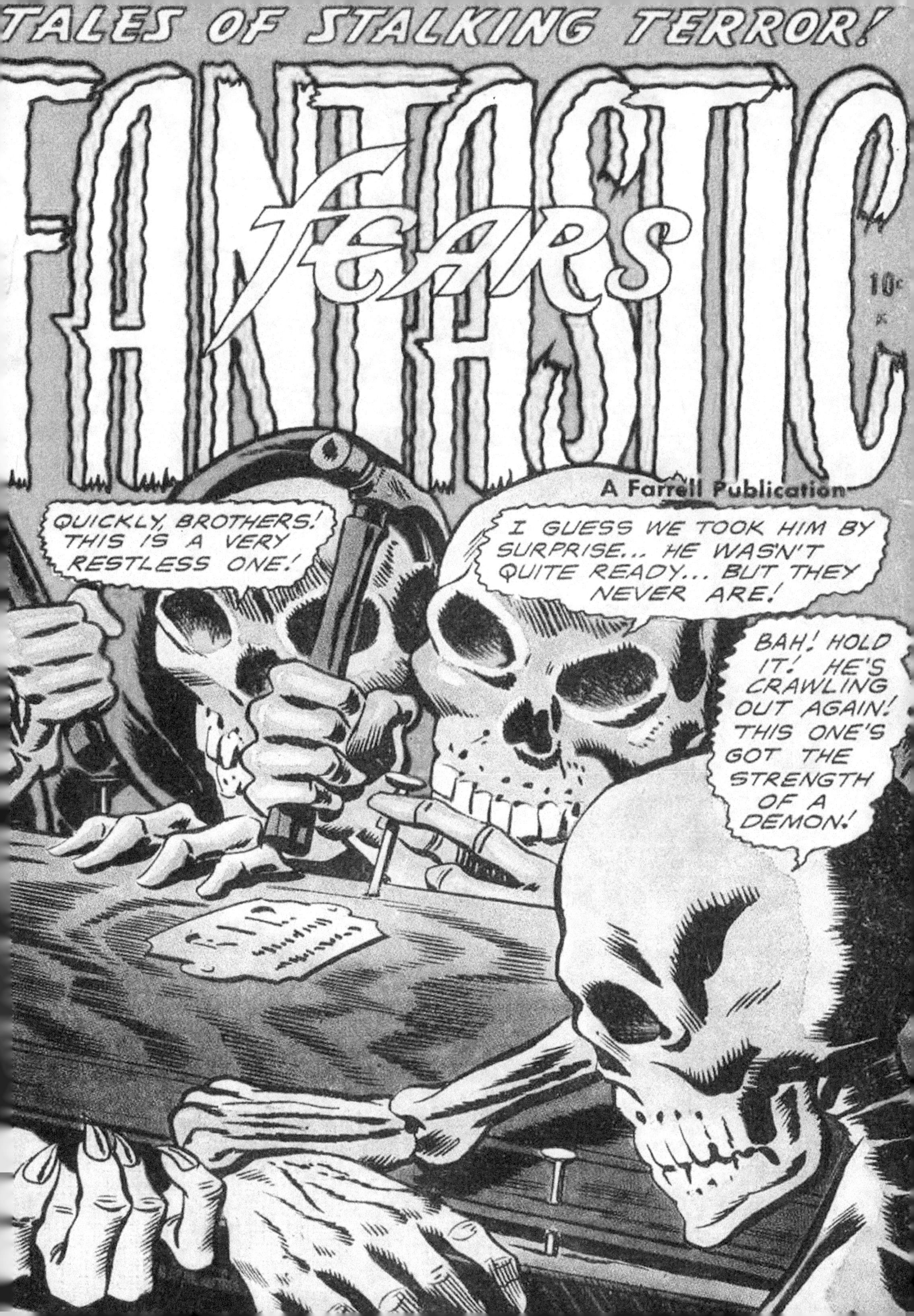

TALES OF STALKING TERROR!
FANTASTIC
FEARS
10¢
A Farrell Publication
QUICKLY, BROTHERS! THIS IS A VERY RESTLESS ONE!
I GUESS WE TOOK HIM BY SURPRISE... HE WASN'T QUITE READY... BUT THEY NEVER ARE!
BAH! HOLD IT! HE'S CRAWLING OUT AGAIN! THIS ONE'S GOT THE STRENGTH OF A DEMON!

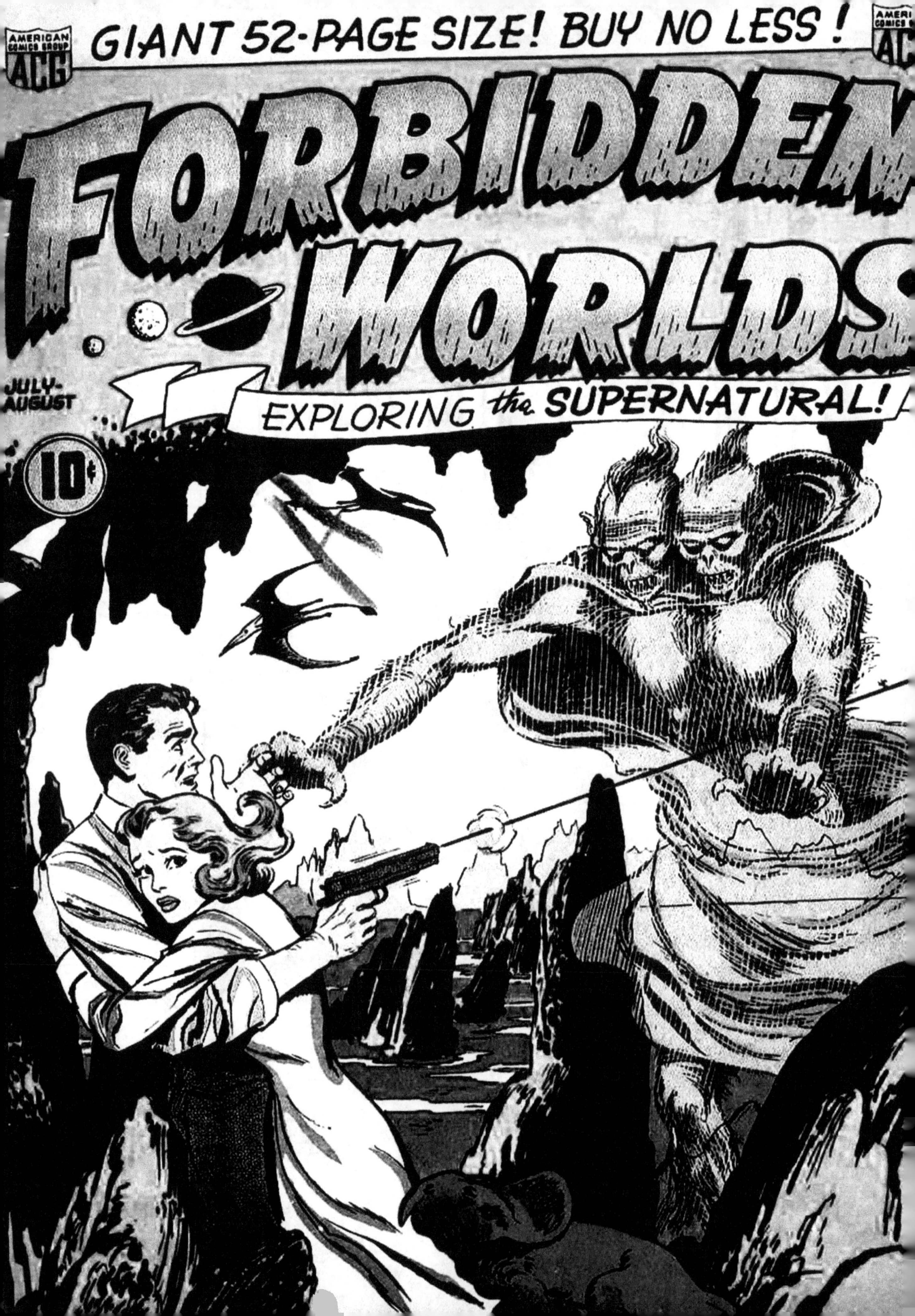

AMERICAN COMICS GROUP
ACG
GIANT 52-PAGE SIZE! BUY NO LESS!
FORBIDDEN WORLDS
JULY-AUGUST
EXPLORING the SUPERNATURAL!
10¢

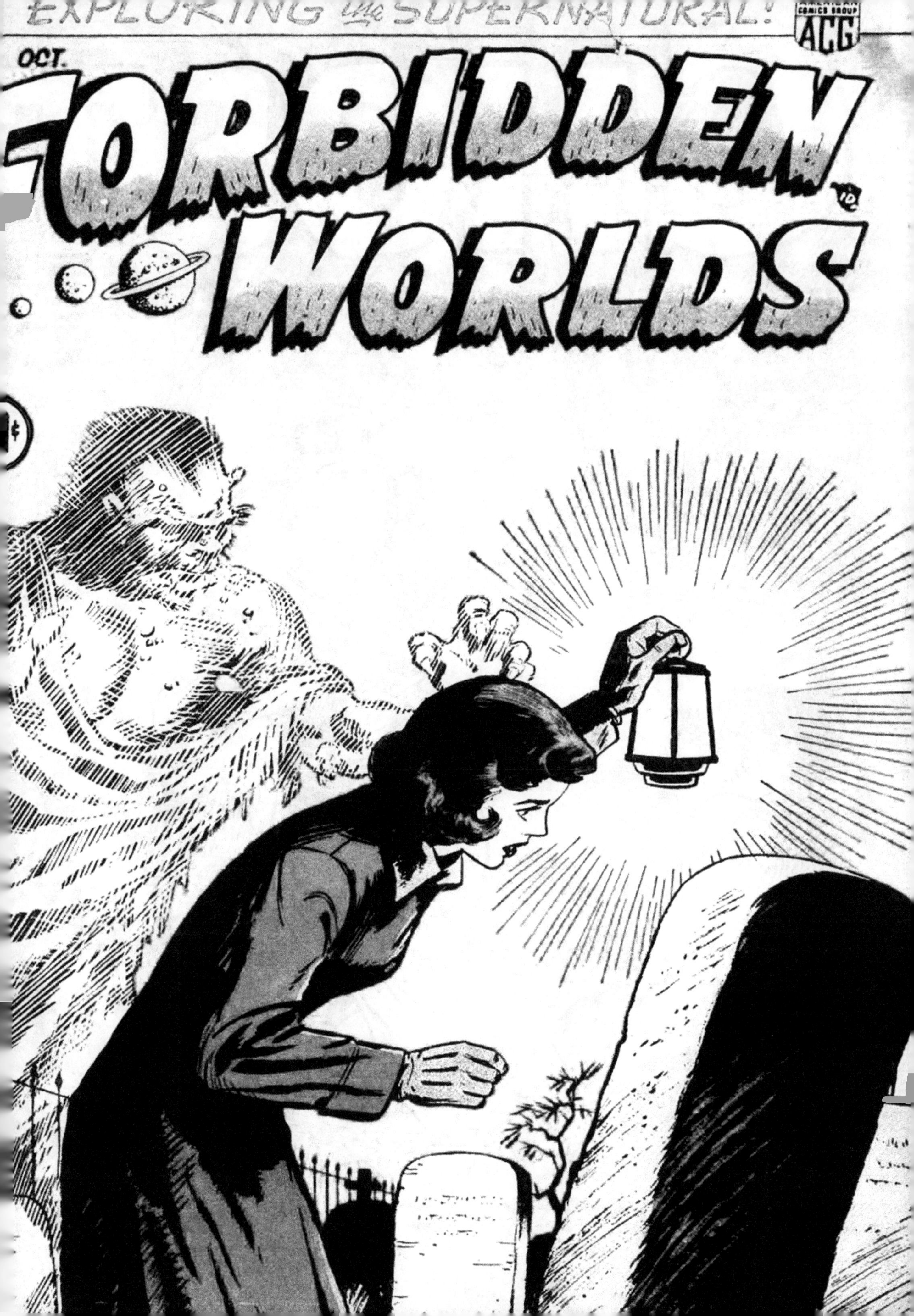
EXPLORING the SUPERNATURAL!
COMICS GROUP
ACG
OCT.
FORBIDDEN WORLDS
10¢

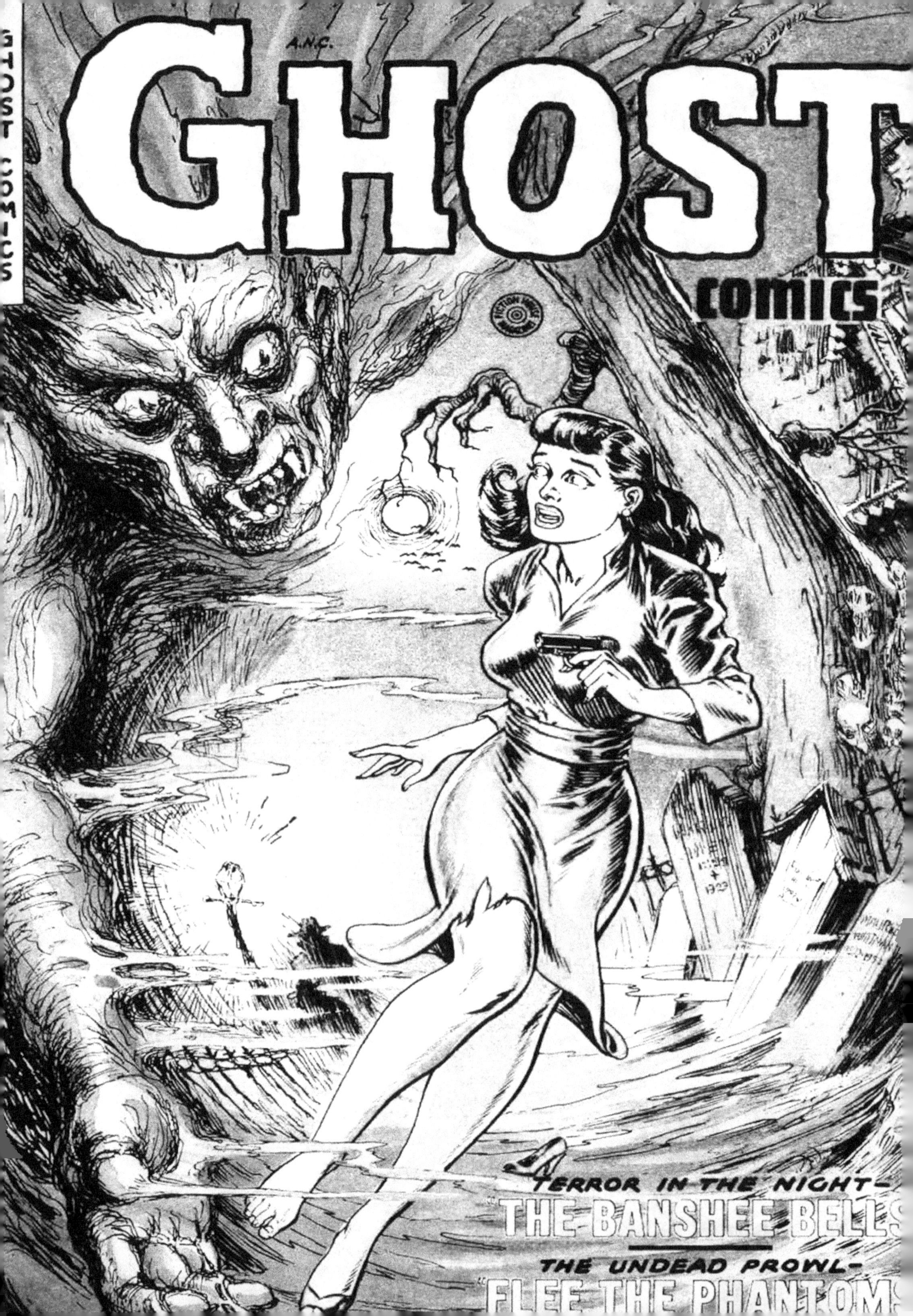
GHOST
COMICS
TERROR IN THE NIGHT-
"THE BANSHEE BELL
THE UNDEAD PROWL-
"FLEE THE PHANTOM

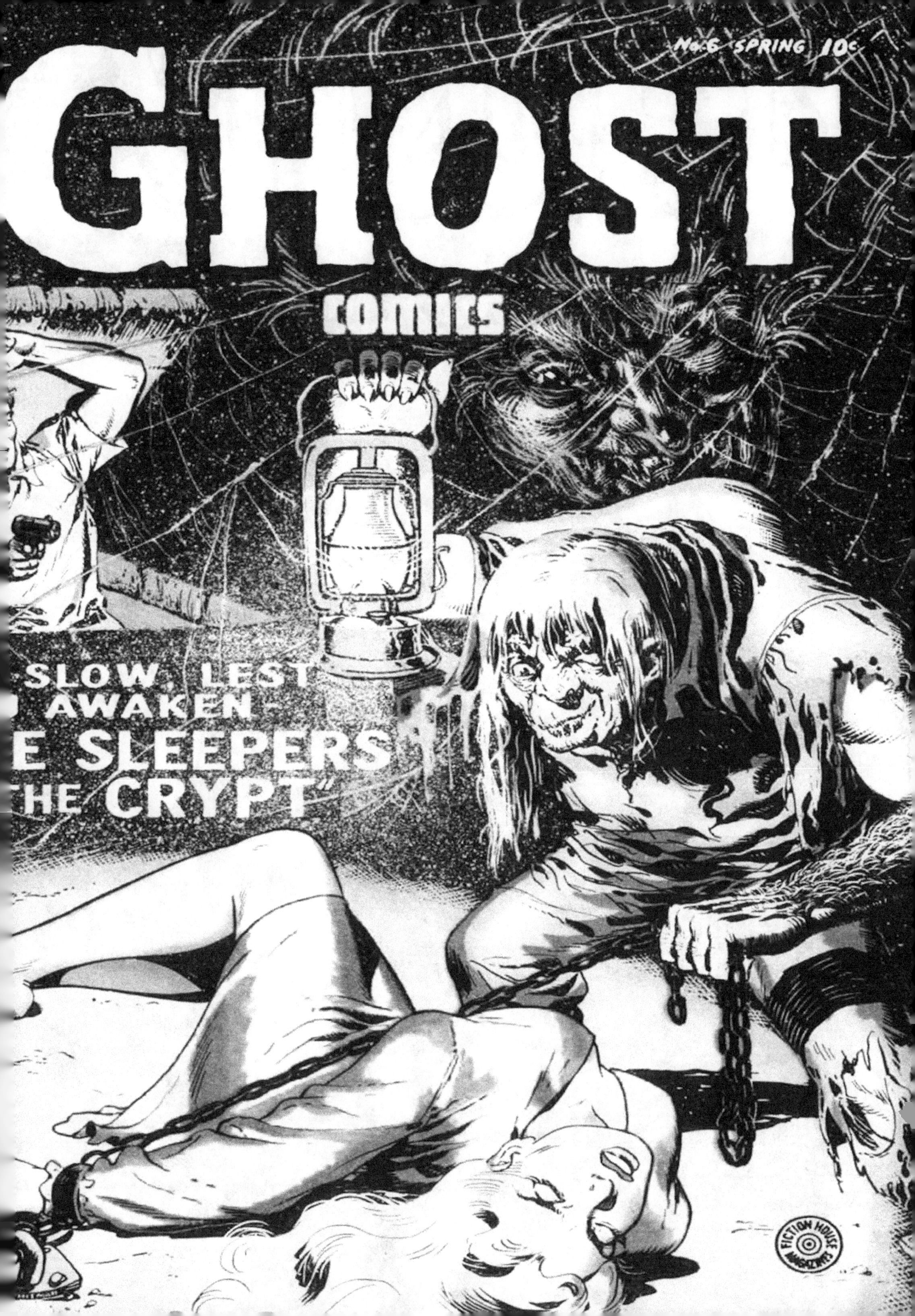
No. 6 SPRING 10¢
GHOST
COMICS
SLOW LEST
AWAKEN
E SLEEPERS
HE CRYPT"
FICTION HOUSE MAGAZINES

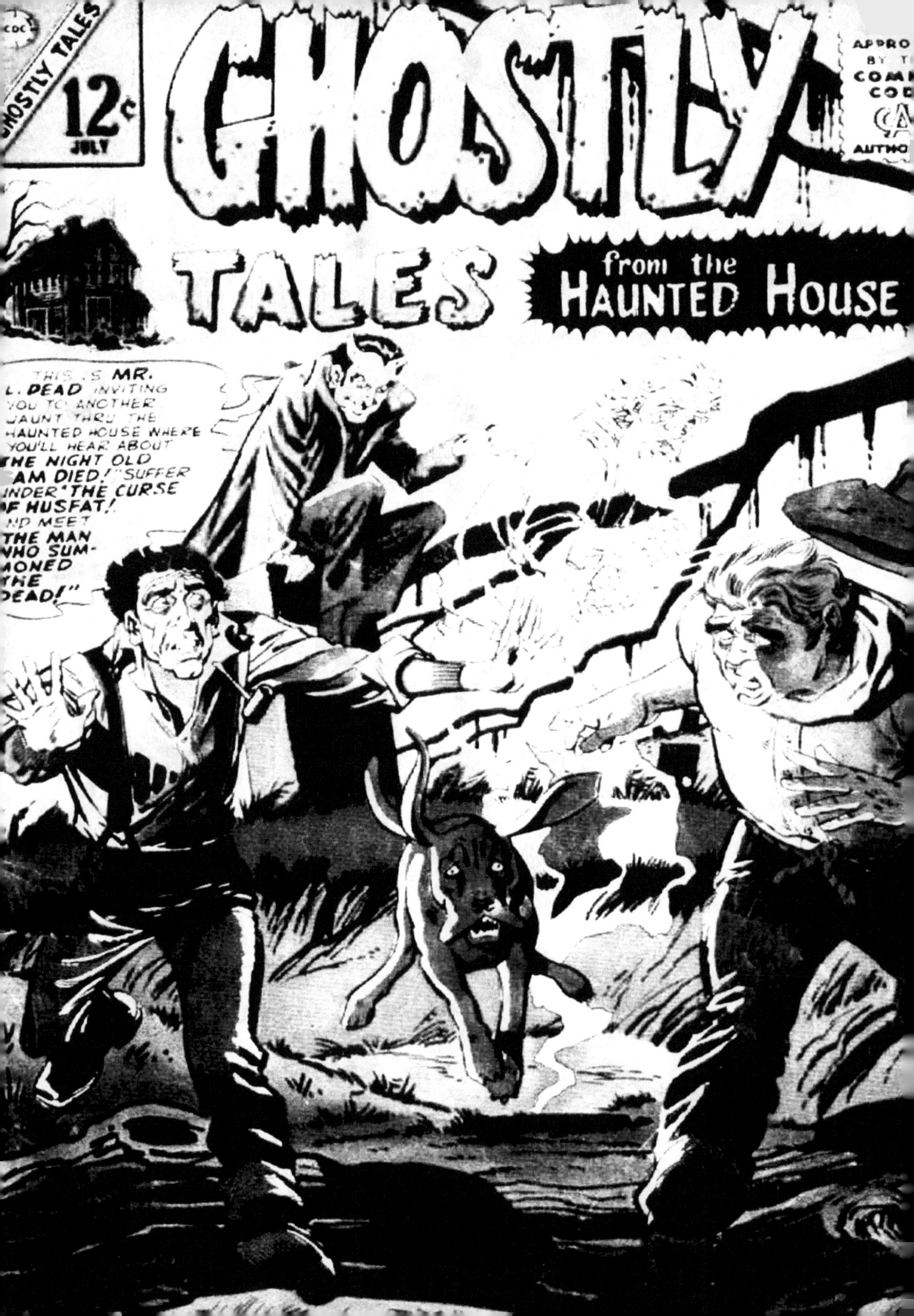
CDC
GHOSTLY TALES
12¢
JULY
GHOSTLY
TALES
from the
HAUNTED HOUSE
THIS IS MR.
L. DEAD INVITING
YOU TO ANOTHER
JAUNT THRU THE
HAUNTED HOUSE WHERE
YOU'LL HEAR ABOUT
THE NIGHT OLD
AM DIED!" "SUFFER
NDER "THE CURSE
F HUSFAT!
ND MEET
THE MAN
HO SUM-
ONED
THE
EAD!"

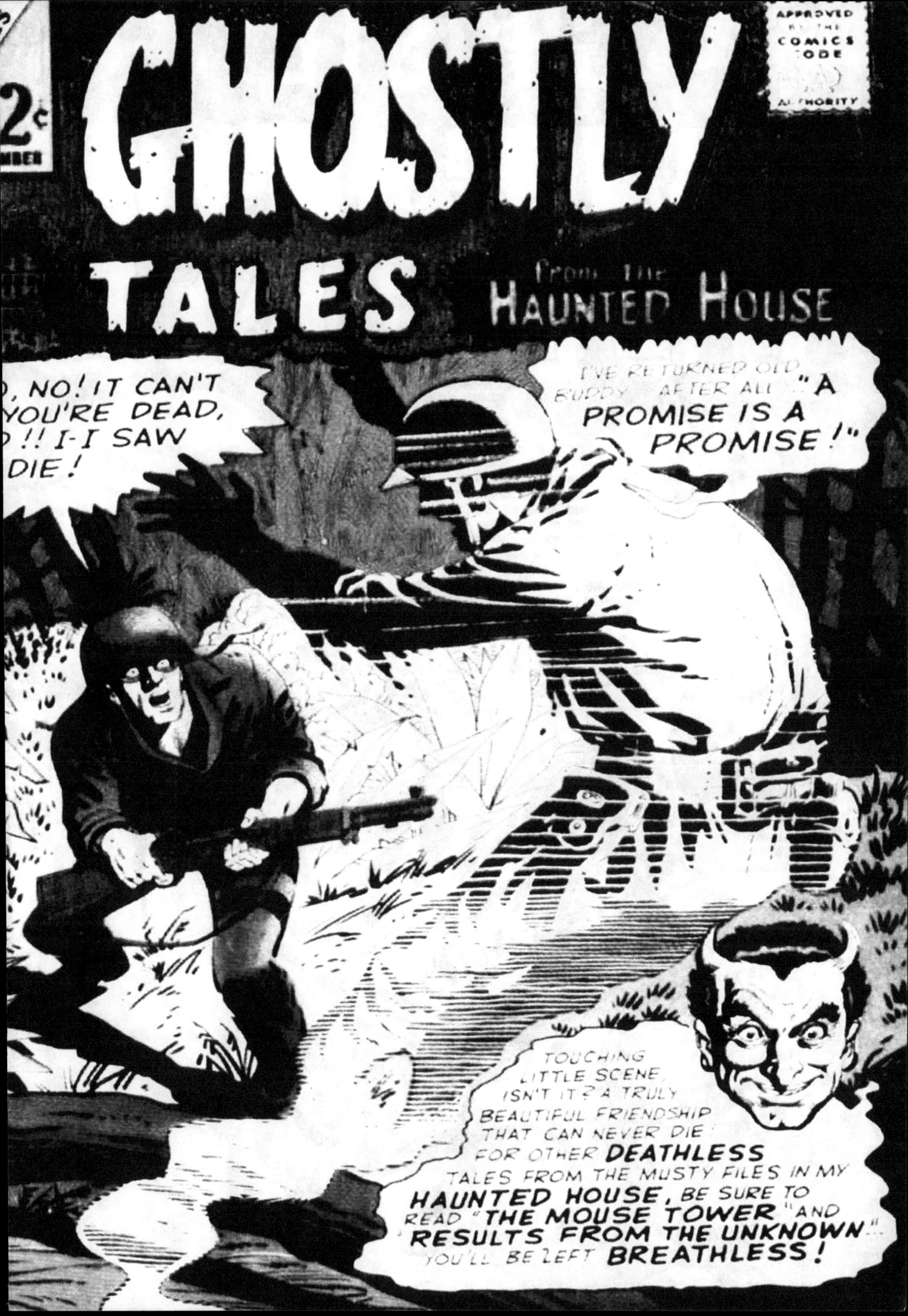12¢
GHOSTLY
TALES
from the HAUNTED HOUSE
APPROVED BY THE COMICS CODE AUTHORITY
, NO! IT CAN'T
YOU'RE DEAD,
!! I-I SAW
DIE!
I'VE RETURNED OLD BUDDY... AFTER ALL... "A PROMISE IS A PROMISE!"
TOUCHING LITTLE SCENE, ISN'T IT? A TRULY BEAUTIFUL FRIENDSHIP THAT CAN NEVER DIE! FOR OTHER DEATHLESS TALES FROM THE MUSTY FILES IN MY HAUNTED HOUSE, BE SURE TO READ "THE MOUSE TOWER" AND "RESULTS FROM THE UNKNOWN"... YOU'LL BE LEFT BREATHLESS!

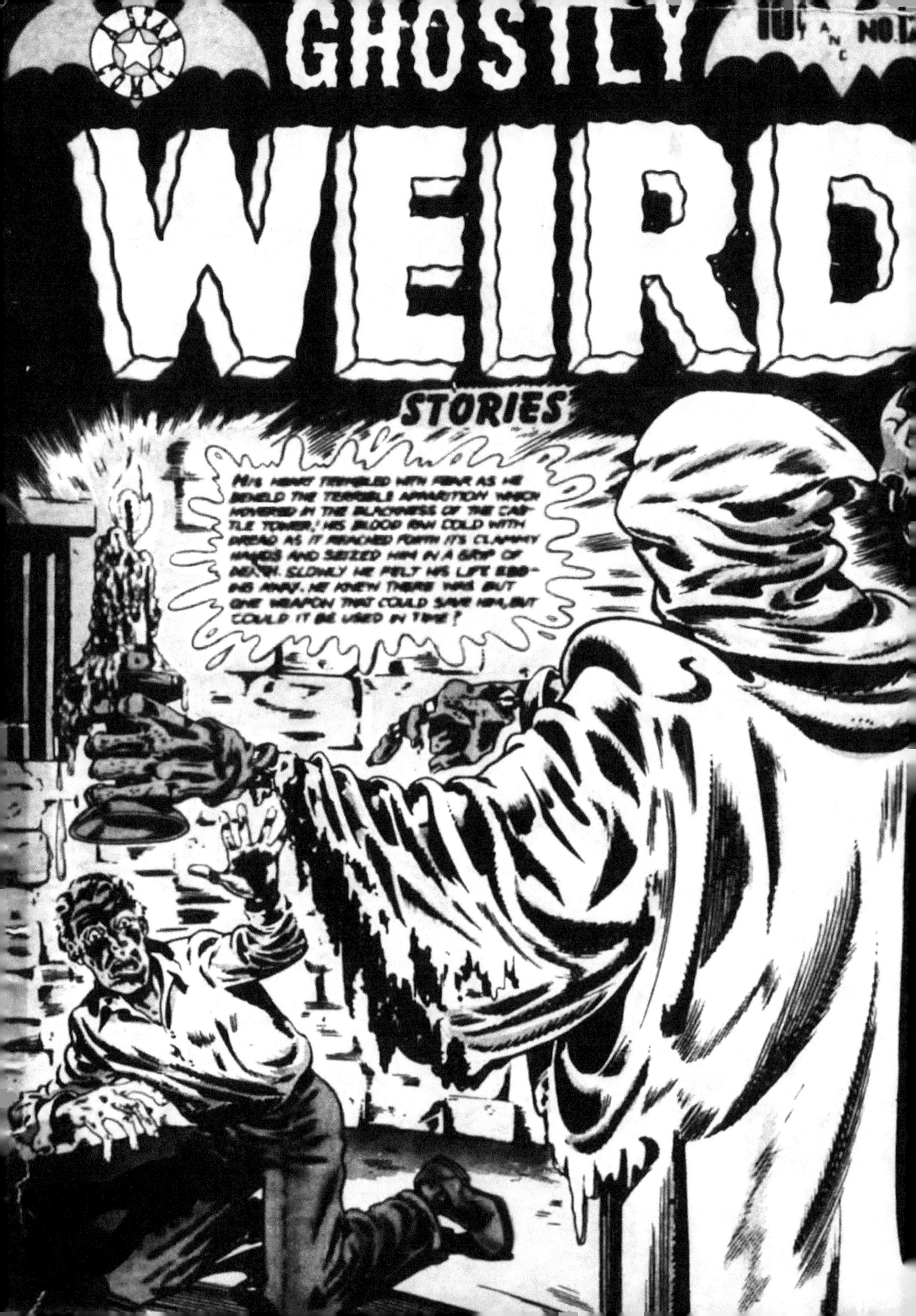
GHOSTLY
WEIRD
STORIES
10¢
JAN C
NO. 1
HIS HEART TREMBLED WITH FEAR AS HE BEHELD THE TERRIBLE APPARITION WHICH HOVERED IN THE BLACKNESS OF THE CASTLE TOWER! HIS BLOOD RAN COLD WITH DREAD AS IT REACHED FORTH ITS CLAMMY HANDS AND SEIZED HIM IN A GRIP OF DEATH. SLOWLY HE FELT HIS LIFE EBBING AWAY. HE KNEW THERE WAS BUT ONE WEAPON THAT COULD SAVE HIM, BUT COULD IT BE USED IN TIME?

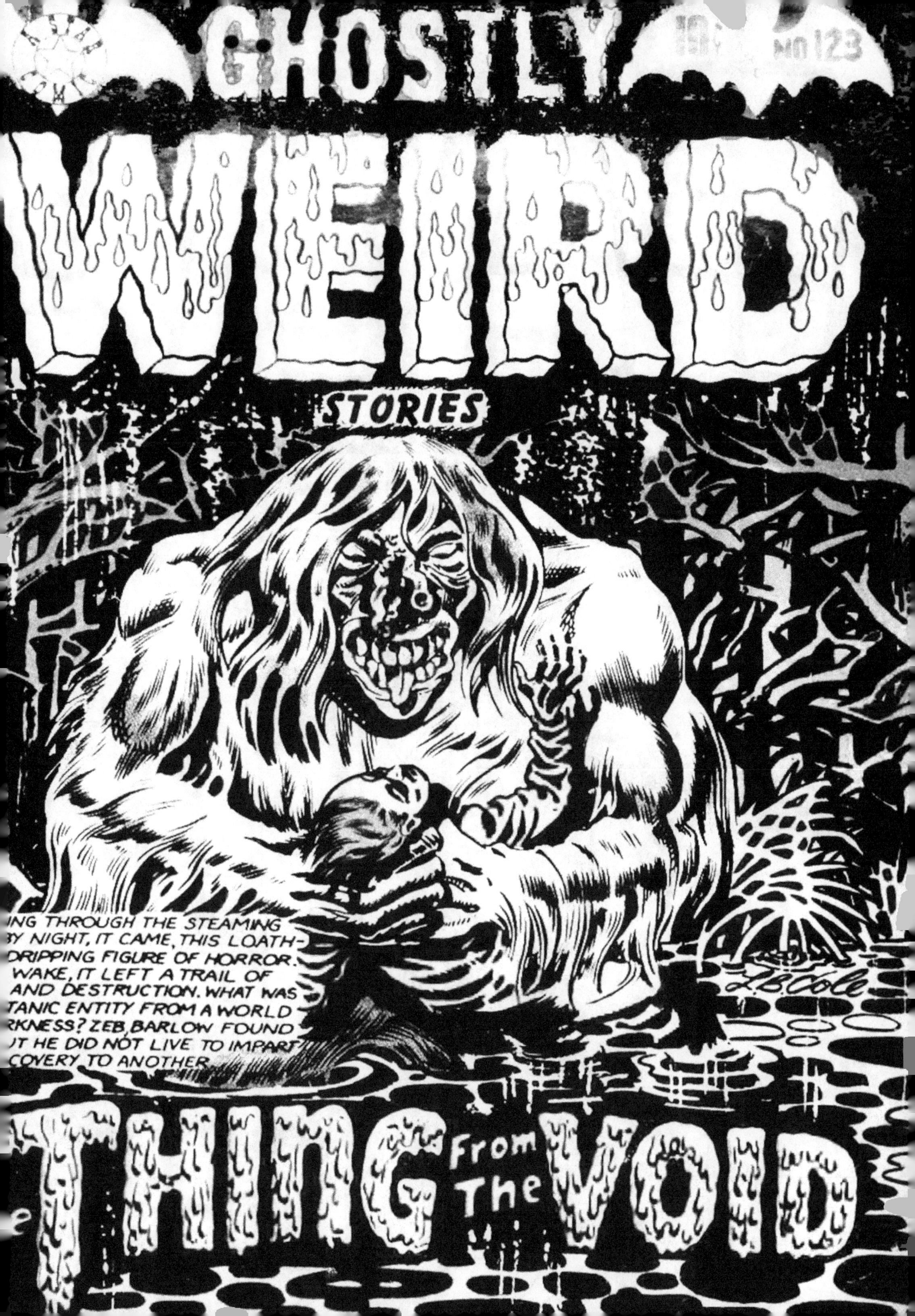
GHOSTLY
NO 123
WEIRD
STORIES
ING THROUGH THE STEAMING
BY NIGHT, IT CAME, THIS LOATH-
DRIPPING FIGURE OF HORROR.
WAKE, IT LEFT A TRAIL OF
AND DESTRUCTION. WHAT WAS
TANIC ENTITY FROM A WORLD
RKNESS? ZEB BARLOW FOUND
UT HE DID NOT LIVE TO IMPART
COVERY TO ANOTHER
L.B. Cole
THING from The VOID

THE HAND OF FATE

FEB.
10c

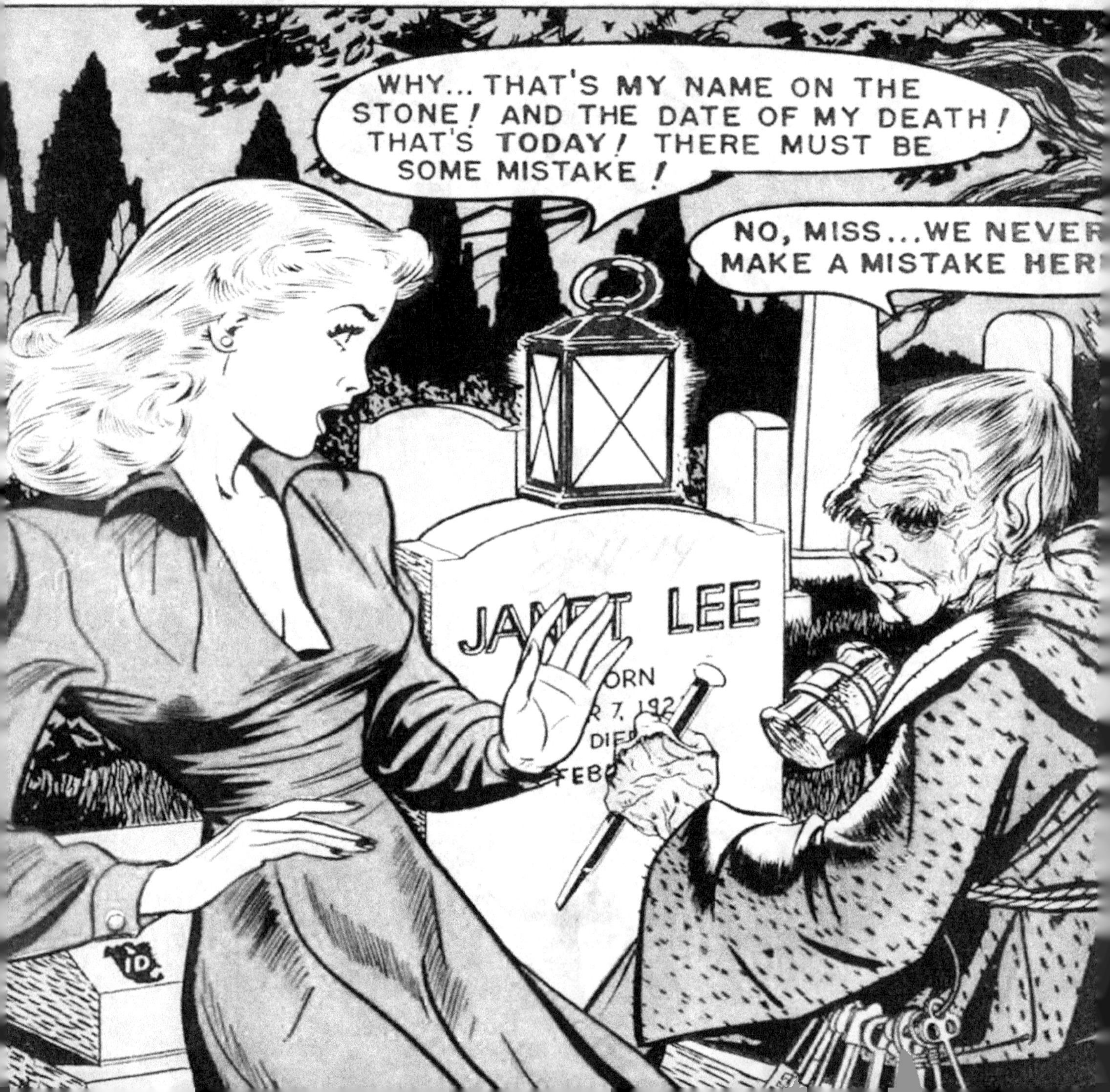
WHY... THAT'S MY NAME ON THE STONE! AND THE DATE OF MY DEATH! THAT'S TODAY! THERE MUST BE SOME MISTAKE!
NO, MISS... WE NEVER MAKE A MISTAKE HER

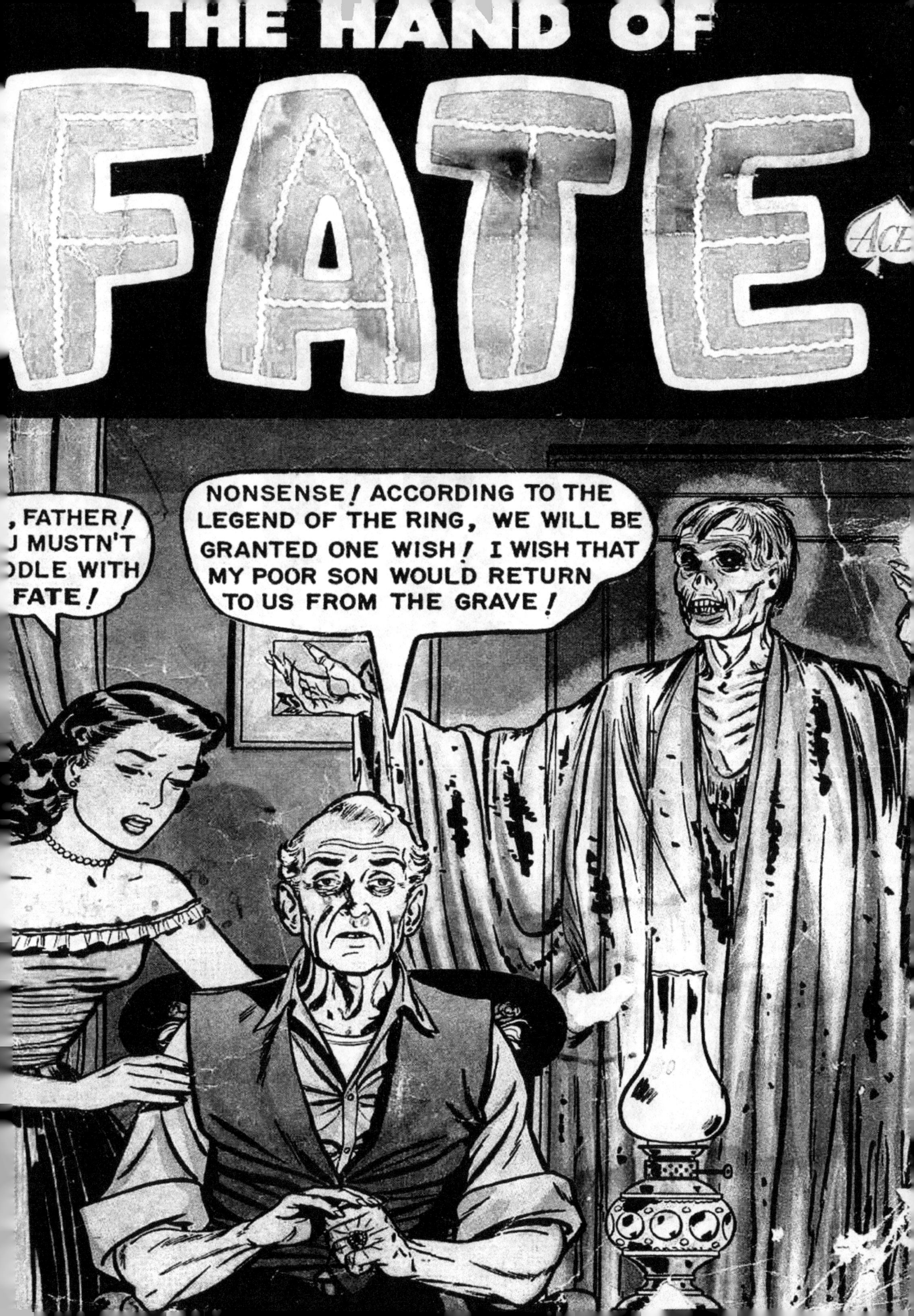
THE HAND OF
FATE
, FATHER! MUSTN'T DDLE WITH FATE!
NONSENSE! ACCORDING TO THE LEGEND OF THE RING, WE WILL BE GRANTED ONE WISH! I WISH THAT MY POOR SON WOULD RETURN TO US FROM THE GRAVE!

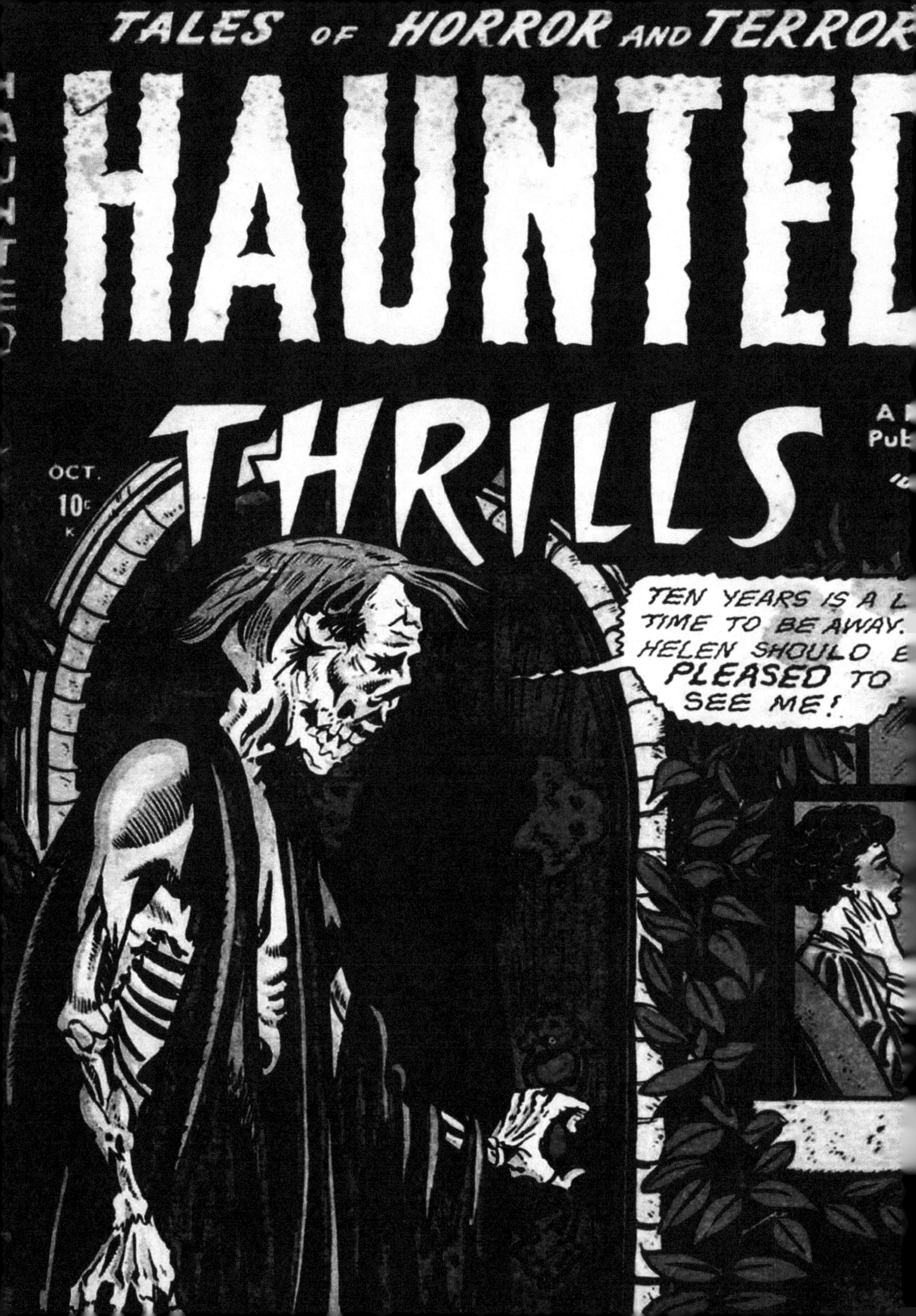
TALES OF HORROR AND TERROR
HAUNTED
THRILLS
OCT.
10¢
TEN YEARS IS A L
TIME TO BE AWAY.
HELEN SHOULD B
PLEASED TO
SEE ME!

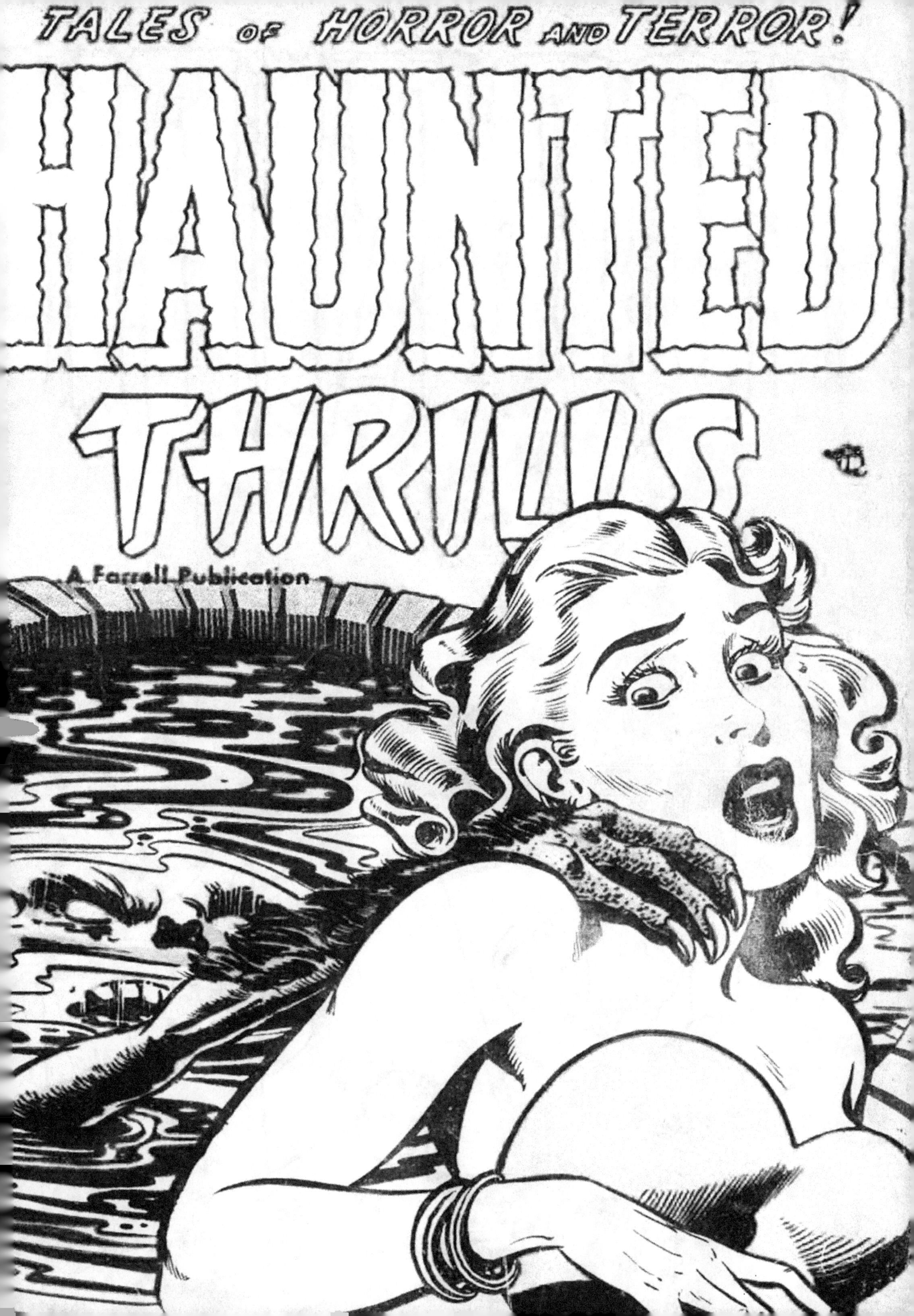
TALES OF HORROR AND TERROR!
HAUNTED THRILLS
A Farrell Publication

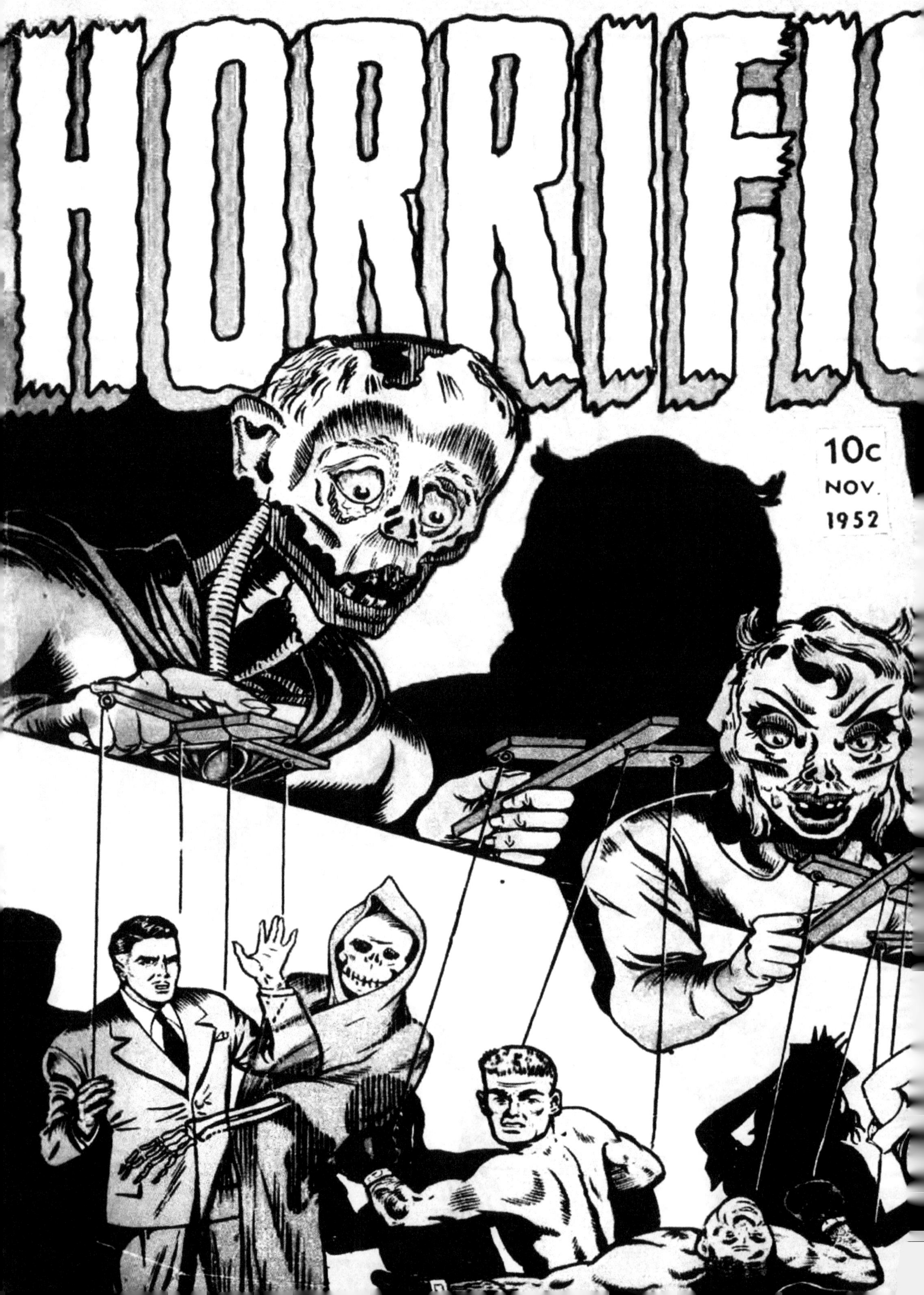
HORRIFIC
10c
NOV.
1952

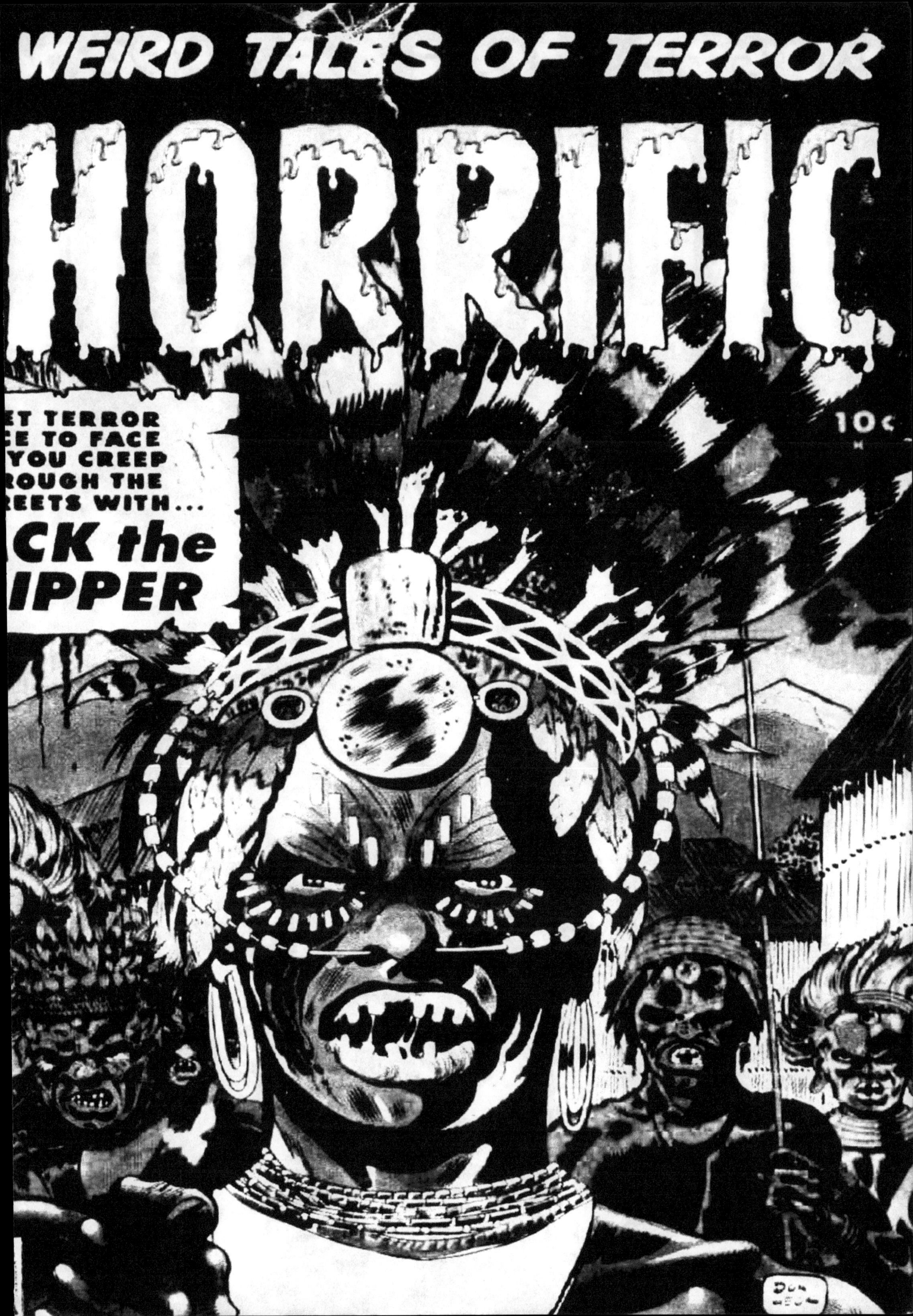
WEIRD TALES OF TERROR
HORRIFIC
ET TERROR
CE TO FACE
YOU CREEP
ROUGH THE
REETS WITH...
CK the
IPPER
10¢

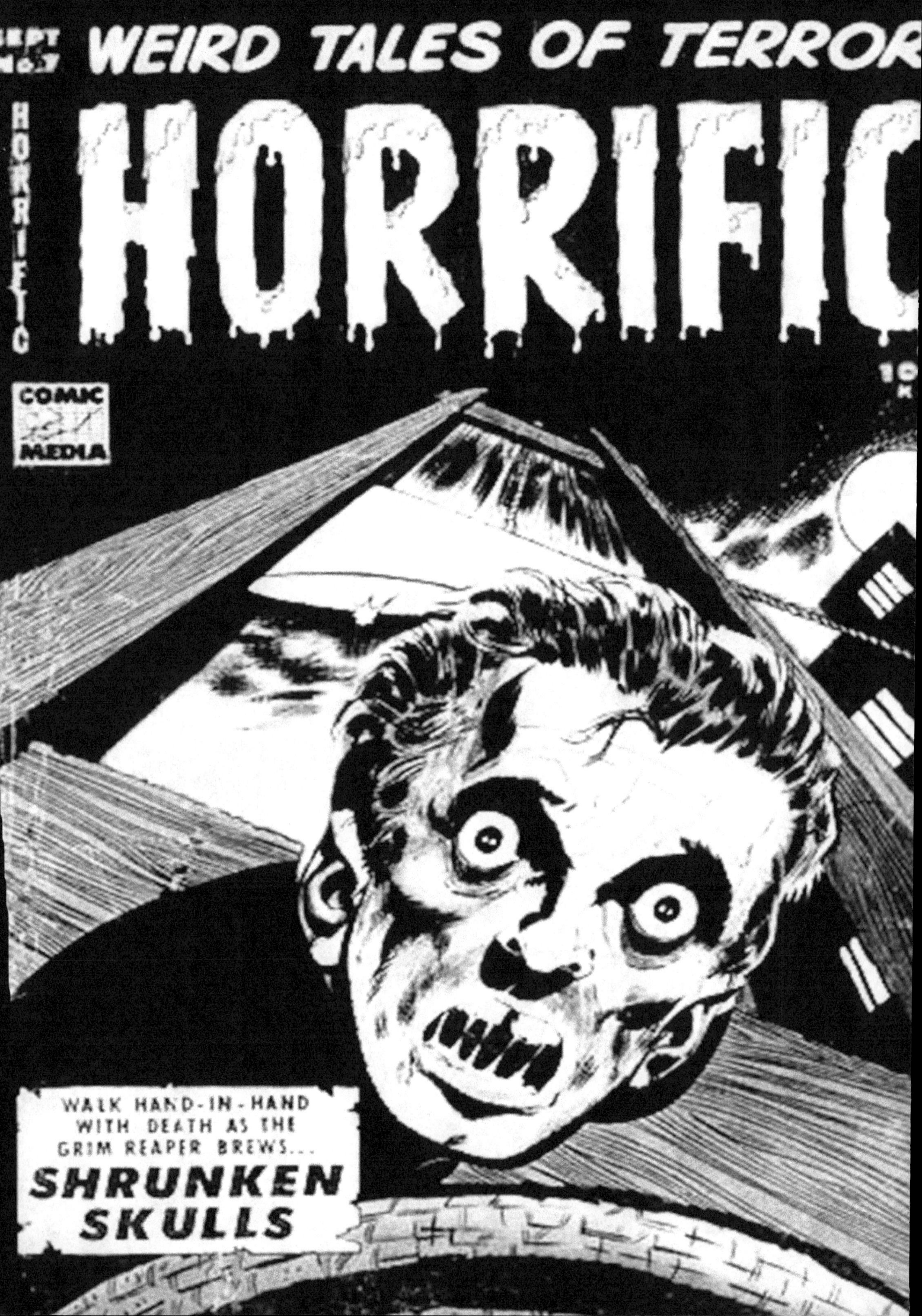

WEIRD TALES OF TERROR
HORRIFIC
HORRIFIC
COMIC MEDIA
WALK HAND-IN-HAND WITH DEATH AS THE GRIM REAPER BREWS...
SHRUNKEN SKULLS

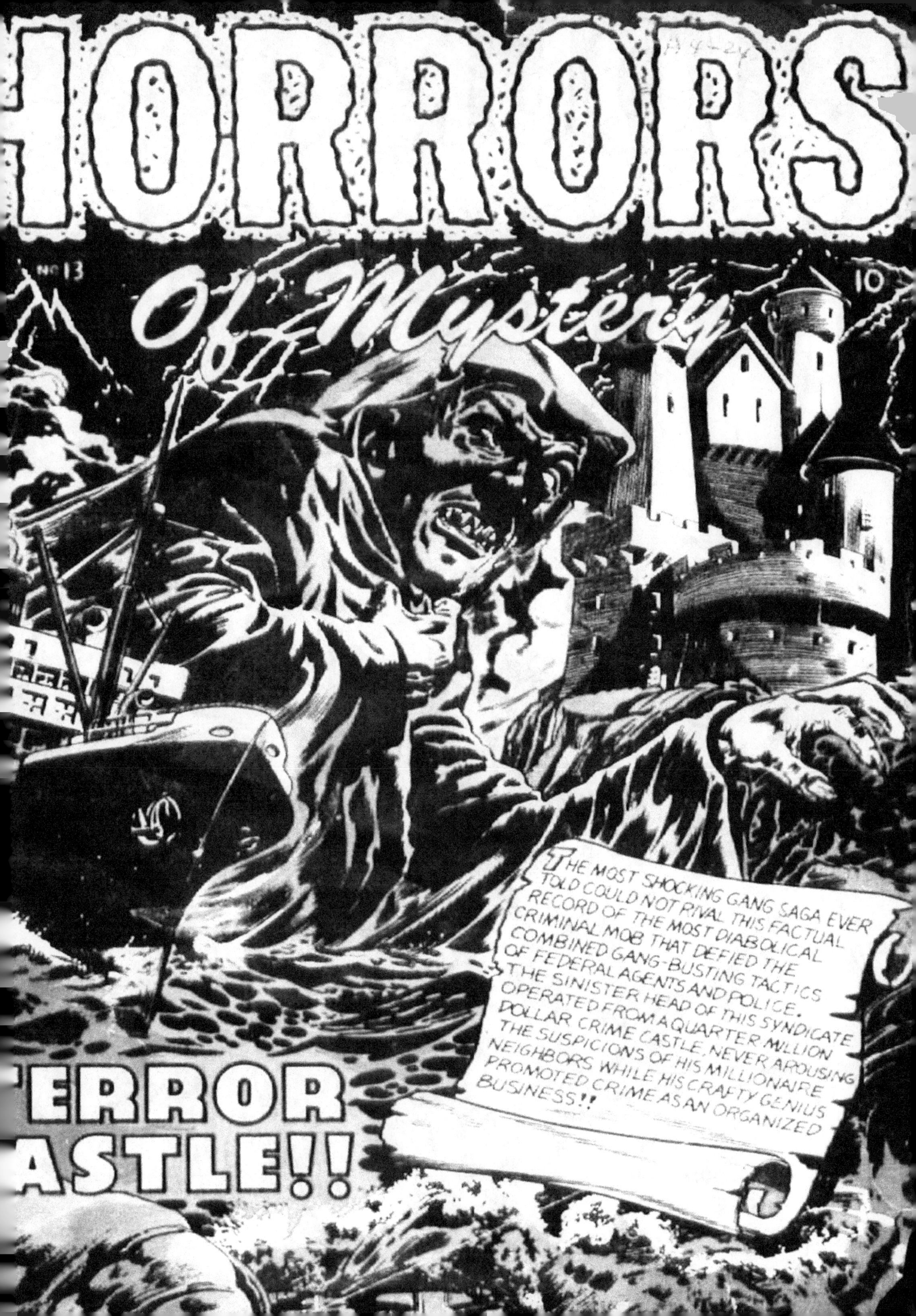
HORRORS
Of Mystery
No 13
10
THE MOST SHOCKING GANG SAGA EVER TOLD COULD NOT RIVAL THIS FACTUAL RECORD OF THE MOST DIABOLICAL CRIMINAL MOB THAT DEFIED THE COMBINED GANG-BUSTING TACTICS OF FEDERAL AGENTS AND POLICE. THE SINISTER HEAD OF THIS SYNDICATE OPERATED FROM A QUARTER MILLION DOLLAR CRIME CASTLE, NEVER AROUSING THE SUSPICIONS OF HIS MILLIONAIRE NEIGHBORS WHILE HIS CRAFTY GENIUS PROMOTED CRIME AS AN ORGANIZED BUSINESS!!
ERROR
ASTLE!!

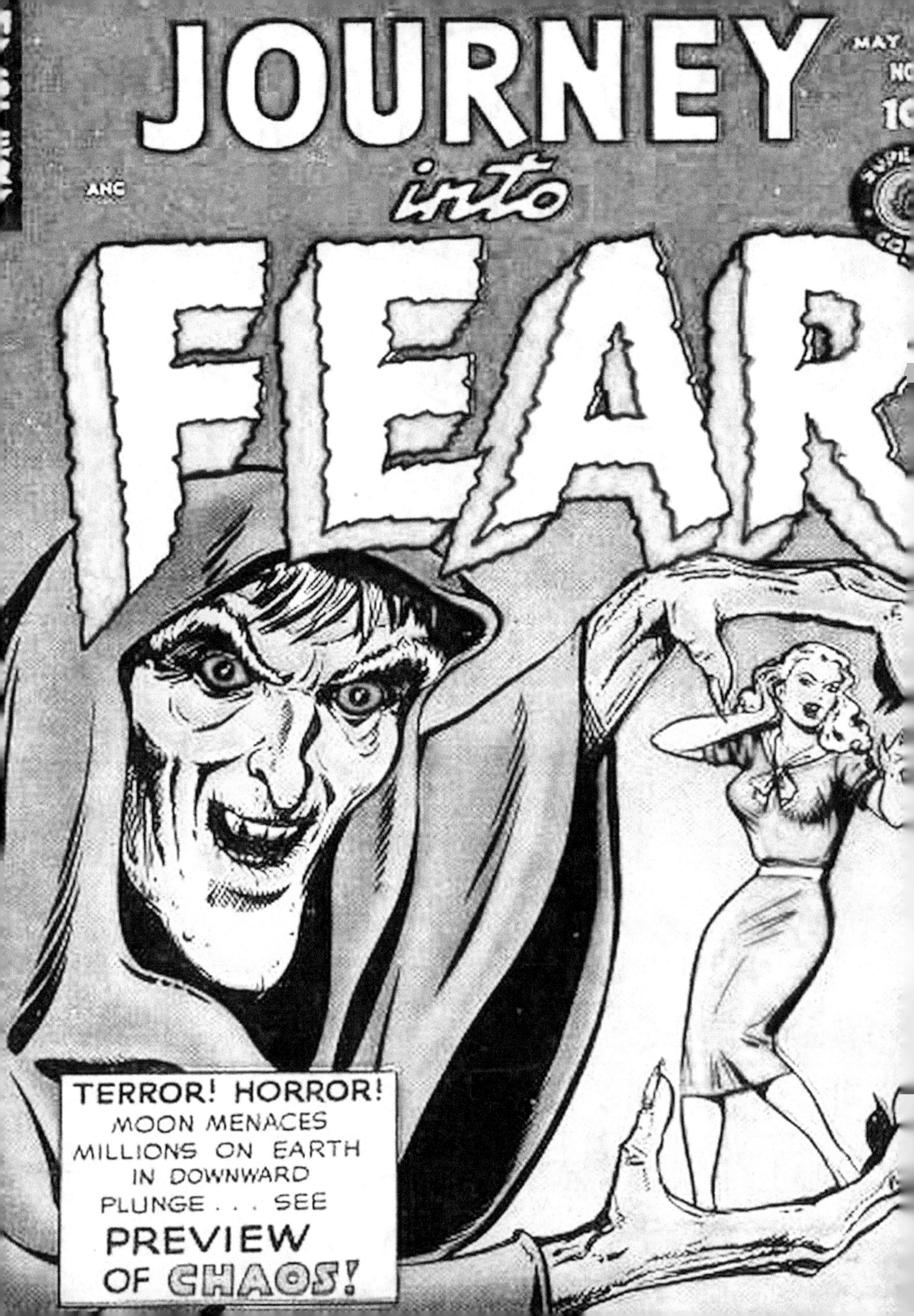

JOURNEY
into
FEAR
ANC
TERROR! HORROR!
MOON MENACES MILLIONS ON EARTH IN DOWNWARD PLUNGE . . . SEE
PREVIEW OF CHAOS!

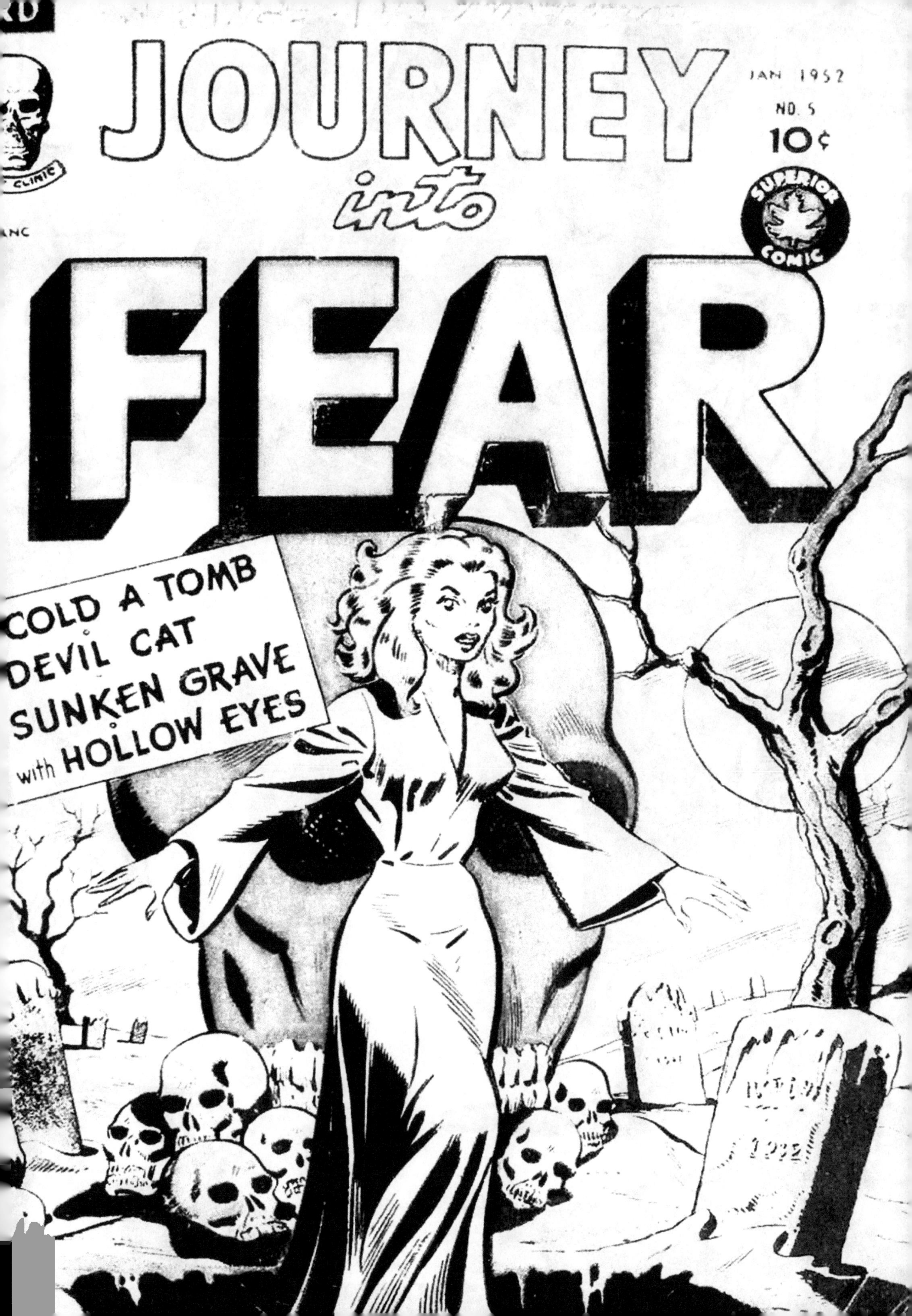

JOURNEY into FEAR
JAN 1952
NO. 5
10¢
SUPERIOR COMIC
COLD A TOMB
DEVIL CAT
SUNKEN GRAVE
SUNKEN GRAVE
with HOLLOW EYES

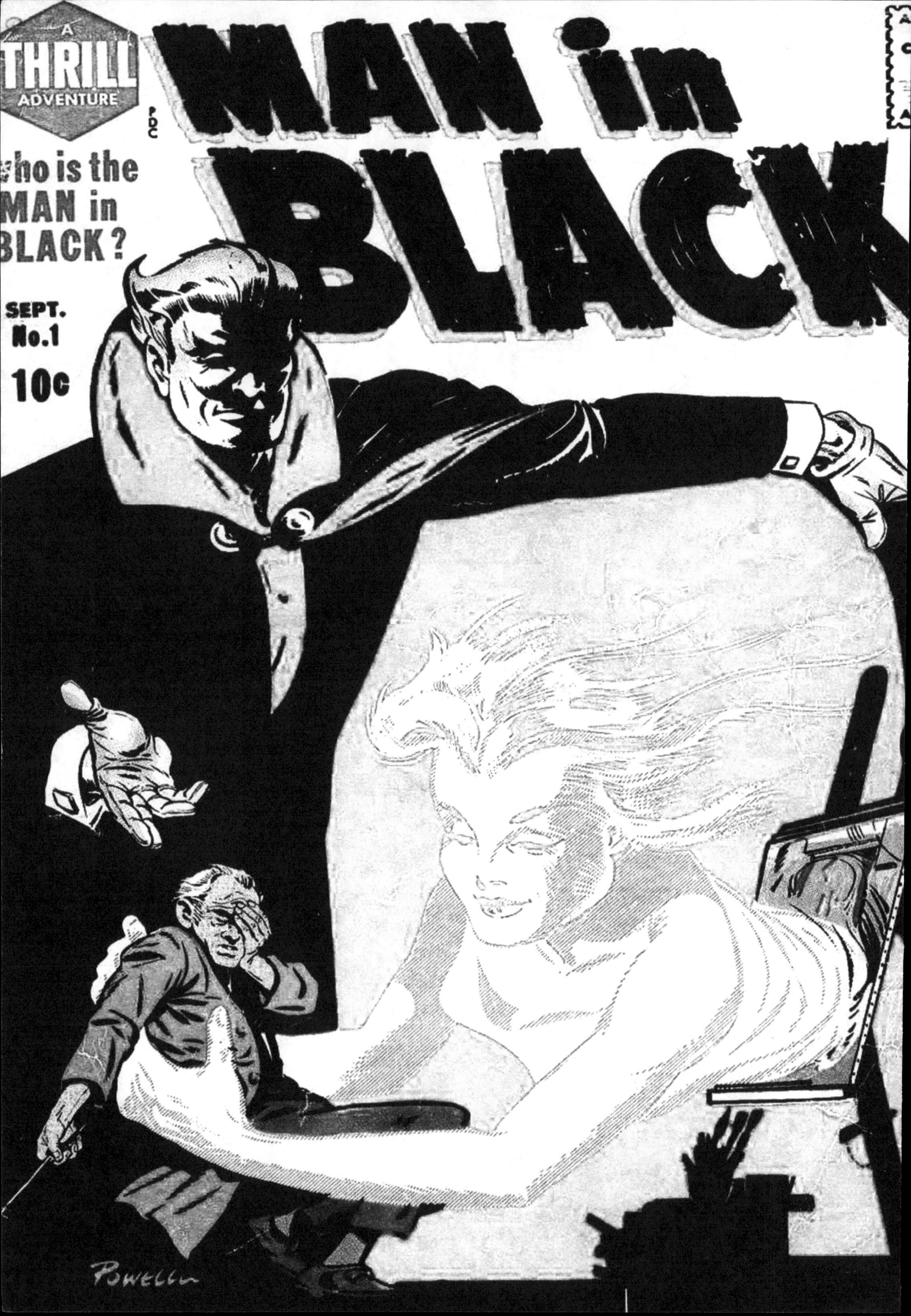

A THRILL ADVENTURE
MAN in BLACK
PDC
who is the MAN in BLACK?
SEPT.
No.1
10¢
Powell

CPSIA information can be obtained
at www.ICGtesting.com
Printed in the USA
BVHW011216310322
632995BV00012B/509

9 781988 369